TEC

A PULP FACTION COMPILATION

PULP FACTION>60 ALEXANDER ROAD>LONDON>N19 3PQ

First published in 1995 by Pulp Faction
60 Alexander Rd, London N19 3PQ

CIP data available from the British Library

ISBN: 1-899571-01-9

Printed in England

Editor: Elaine Palmer
Art Editor: Daniel Mogford
Contributing Artist: Christopher Harris [Pagan Da
Contributing Editors: Robyn Conway, Darren Benne
Thanks to: Tim Spencer for C a [illegible] ,
Huw Morgan for Garandahand
Francis Stebbing for Lungfat
Cover design: Daniel Mogford

PULP Faction wishes to thank: The London Arts Board, The Paul Hamlyn Foundation, Lowenbrau UK Ltd, Time Out, Islington Council; also John Hampson, Jeff Noon, Kirsty at Ringpull, Geoff Davis, Bettina Walter, Fabian Monheim, Nana Ya Mensah, Jo Gatt, Paul Curry and Nina Kapur.

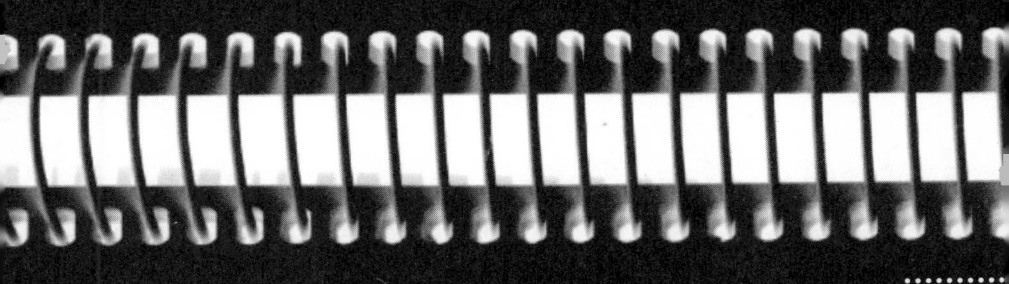

contents

CITY of FUSION

nicholas royle

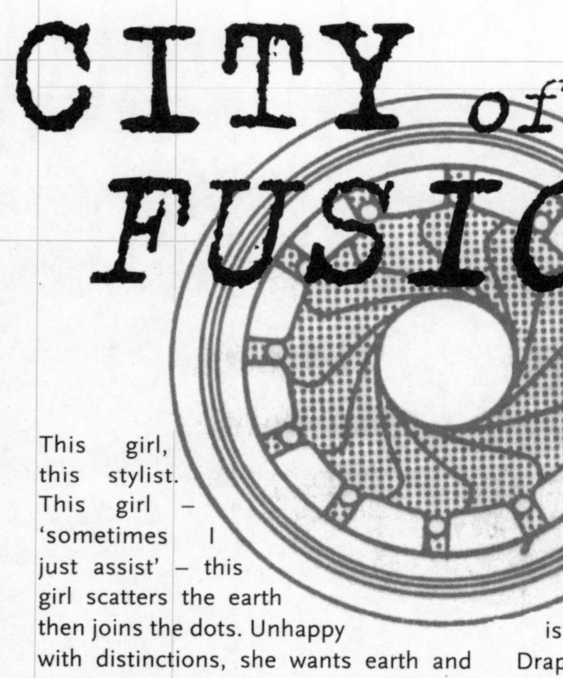

This girl, this stylist. This girl – 'sometimes I just assist' – this girl scatters the earth then joins the dots. Unhappy with distinctions, she wants earth and sky to be one. Style and content the same thing. This girl, this... *girl*.

She's in, at last she's in. She floats up to the reception desk. More flight deck than reception desk, all frosted glass, underlighting and height. All bullshit. You've practically to stand on tiptoes. She loses the book, stands it on the floor, leaning against her leg. *Book*. Some book. Some stories it tells with its *pictures*.

She flicks her hair behind her ear, then does it again before it could possibly have fallen back. She knows. She's knows she's doing it, she knows how it looks. No one's watching. She glances round: the only creature with manners to raise an eye in her direction is the camera for the CCTV.

'I've come to see Jim Cover. I've got an appointment,' she says. Like that's his name, his real name. Some name for an art director. Just like that guy she saw last week at *Dazed & Confused* was really called Jefferson Hack. A journalist, an editor. Yeah, sure. And Nigel Draper runs the curtains franchise at Harrods.

She hears someone ask her for her name. She looks down, meets the girl's eye, tells her what it is. 'Eleven o'clock,' she adds. 'And I have got other meetings.' Just a little white lie. It has taken months to get this one, to get this far. Months of phone calls, disappointing shoots, more phone calls. Months of joining the dots. Literally months.

The girl gives her a badge saying VISITOR. Yeah, right.

'Take the lift to the eighth floor,' she says. 'He'll meet you there.'

She turns, viscose slip dress catching on her arse. She likes that, likes knowing the girl at reception is still watching her, wishing she had an arse like that. Or a dress like that.

The lift doors close. She checks out the mirror. Eight floors of mirror time – what a treat, a rare treat. But it's got a kind of tacky bronze sheen to it. Like the mirrors in the Ladies' at Singapore Airport, they had something on them, or in the lights. They did something, performed some kind of sorcery. Only in Singapore they did it to flatter you, make you looked tanned. Here the intention is the opposite. Do they use the stairs or what, these people? Thinking about Singapore brought back thoughts of André.

The twat.

She'd told André about the mirrors, tried to drag him into the Ladies'. For a self-confessed rebel he was terrified of overstepping the mark. Wouldn't go in with her. Told her it was the same in the Gents'. Probably was. He was still a twat. He'd wandered round the airport with his hand shading his mouth and chin because he'd heard they didn't allow beards in Singapore. What did he think they were going to do, come and give him a shave? Yeah, right.

When the lift doors open there's a guy waiting for her. He's holding a can of Coke.

'Yeah, hi,' he says to her shoulder. 'Through here. You've brought your book.'

She follows him. He stops by the newspaper-strewn table to grab a cigarette from someone else's pack. Flicks open a Zippo lighter. Imitation (like André's). She lugs her great book after him to the couches. There are three huge couches, set in an unfinished square. He sits down on the edge of a cushion, spreads his legs.

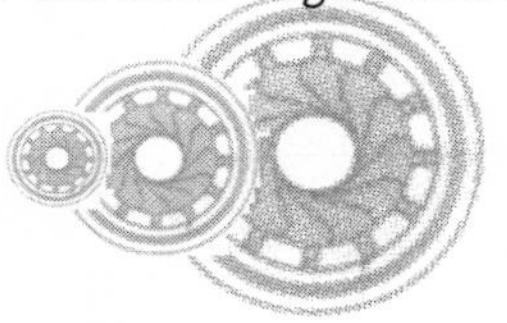

His cigarette winks out, he didn't light it very well. As he lifts the *faux* Zippo again she hears the conversation of three women sitting round the table behind her. Their disembodied voices are punctuated by cigarette sucks and newspaper flicks.

'You know, he's sort of small and Woody Allenish, if you like that sort of thing,' one of them is saying.

'For fuck's sake,' says another.

He's waiting for her, chugging his Coke. She lifts the book up off the floor, slides it across her slippery lap into his. He supports it on his knees, undoes the zip, opens it. Doesn't speak as he turns the huge, plastic pages. The photos are good, she knows they are. They're very good. No worries there.

'I, like, you know...' she says.

'Yeah.'

He turns over, takes a drag on his Camel, swallows some Coke. There's some sort of colourless substance running out of his nose like snail slime. He's turning the pages quite quickly, his eyes sliding across the images: the shimmering silks on Canvey Island, the Oakley sunglasses in Subterania (she knows someone who knows someone who supplies crap doves to the girl who sleeps with the guy on the door), the hooded tops in St George's Gardens.

Is he looking properly?

'Here, you know... I don't know...' Her hand slews across the image, pointing at something which she knows signifies nothing. It's all a game, only this guy always gets to roll twice.

'Yeah, right... Interesting.' He nods, sucks on his fag, turns the page.

She can see sunlight shafting through the bristles stuck on his chin like surviving spines on an ancient hairbrush. This fashion for goatees that aren't even goatees, this fashion, this... pitiful sheep mentality. Fuck 'em.

'Sometimes I just assist.'

Why? Why did she say it?

Right at the nadir she gives in, exactly when she's at her most vulnerable she lies down and says come and fuck me.

And fuck her they do, invariably.

Like when she met André: she was down, very down, after a drug thing with those two boys from Latimer Road. They were dropping tabs of acid like they were Shreddies. Whole fucking bowlfuls. And then they went up on to the Hammersmith & City line at Goldhawk Road. Yeah, right. Good idea. Get down on to the track and take a walk. Nice one. Fine until you've got trains coming from both directions. The two boys had it all timed and they ducked out, escaped into the BBC somehow. She heard later they were arrested in the middle of the pitch at Loftus Road like the end of some disappointing 60s movie. Carrying? The filth, in a rare shaft of constabulary wit, said they were surprised they could stand up they were carrying so much stuff. Pockets crammed with narcotics. Acid, Es, powder, barbs – some German stuff the Shepherd's Bush bobbies said they'd never even seen before. And these guys patrol the White City Estate.

Maybe she was lucky that night, although it was hard to see it that way at the time. After narrowly missing point blank impact with several Circle line trains (funny how when you want one you can wait for fucking ages, but when you're wandering down the middle of the track off your face on LSD there's one every two minutes), she thought it would be a neat idea to lie down on the ballast between the tracks with her right leg an inch from one of the live rails. Yeah, right. She was just lucky the next driver to come along was awake and already applying the brakes for Ladbroke Grove.

Somehow she got off virtually scot free on that occasion, unless you counted André. She went to some kind of rehab clinic – not her idea but her parole officer's. And there he was, just the kind of boy she liked. Short and Israeli-looking with army fatigues and scrag end of beard. Like he'd been planted there by whoever was in charge of Ironic Twists of Fate. And when he asked her what her name was and she heard herself saying 'Lilith' after a Ramsey Campbell story she'd read as a little girl, she saw his dark little eyes light up. For whatever reason, that sealed it. 'Lilith,' he whispered and that did it for her.

As soon as she makes the comment about assisting, even the low level of interest Cover has been evincing vanishes altogether.

He flips through the remaining pages. She makes a half-hearted attempt to puff up her dawn shoot on the Thames foreshore by Bankside Power Station, but the moment, if it was ever within her grasp, has gone. Gone like all the others. Cover is just another art director, just another bored coke-head manipulative bastard looking for an excuse to tell her to fuck off.

She realises he's saying something as he zips up the book and passes it back to her. Something that doesn't quite fit.

'I'd be interested to see more,' he's saying and she doesn't know whether to believe him or rub ash in his beard. There's an ashtray on the table but he's been flicking on to the floor, constantly, as they speak.

'You wanna see some more?' she hears herself asking.

'Yeah,' he sucks on a burning filter. 'I'd be interested to see more.'

It's just shit to get rid of her. Surely. But he doesn't need to. He could just tell her to go away and never come back. They do, don't they.

No, they don't. They say they'd be interested to see more. Because they know that one day, in the far future, these young no-hopers will be discovered by someone else and become young turks, and *they'll* be the old farts who never took them seriously. It all comes back to number one.

She stands up, takes the weight of her book.

'Yeah, right,' she says.

He drops his filter on the floor, prods it unnecessarily with his toe. It's a gesture. He doesn't miss a trick. But neither does she. He grunts, looks towards the lift.

'I can manage,' she says and is away. She only has to wait a second or two before the lift arrives. When she glances back before stepping in, he's back at the table where the three women are, helping himself to another cigarette. One of the women shakes her head as if to get hair out of her face, but her hair's cropped to the bone. Fag in hand, elbow on the table, putdown on her painted lips.

She gets in the lift, goes down through the building, past all those minor copies of Jim Cover, those insincere, miserable shadows of their own pathetic and unrealisable ambition. Fuck 'em.

Yeah. Right.

Every year around mid-June, at least since she met André, she – this girl, this stylist, this *Lilith* – gets jittery. In fact, it's been happening for years, since before the André episode. Which was why, when he explained everything to her, it all made such perfect sense. It had always been, or so it *now* seemed with the benefit of hindsight, some sort of big, grown-up version of PMT. Jittery she'd get but also full of excitement and anxiety. Unformed anxiety. Until André. Anxiety without a nucleus around which to coalesce. Like water vapour without dust motes about which to condense. So there could be no rain, no release of tension. Until, one day, she'd realise the tension had gone. She'd get up in the morning and maybe it had rained in the night. Summer rain. Midsummer rain. Big fat blotches on the pavement flags. A smell in the air like no other. Summer rain. Midsummer rain.

André told her about midsummer. She wanted to know how midsummer could arrive so early on in what we perceive as being summer, but he told her not to be so 'fucking dense'.

'From this moment on,' he told her as they climbed up Primrose Hill on a rare tranquil evening, 'the forces of light wane and continue to do so until the sun starts to wax again.'

She can still remember that night. André was more considerate and solicitous to her that night than at any other point in their relationship. He told her as she leant through the gradually darkening air towards the summit that she resembled a swan. She was wearing her viscose slip dress with spaghetti straps from Koh Samui – the same dress she wears now as she lugs her portfolio from magazine to magazine – which she'd only acquired days before. She'd got it to use in a shoot and liked it so much she hung on to it. Never in fact used it. She did something with papery soft jerkins from Errol Peake instead. The model, an androgynous black girl from North Kensington recommended by a friend of a friend, tried hitting on her, which she found kind of weird but flattering. She pretended she hadn't understood but let the girl keep the jerkin – 120 quid's worth. (Saw her again at a party in Kensal Rise and the girl, still wearing the jerkin and hanging on the arm of Andrea Dworkin's stunt double, stiffed her.)

She still thinks about the swan thing, the single remaining shred of evidence that André wasn't a complete prick.

Two days after her humiliation at the hands of Jim Cover, she's at a party in Soho. Some production company. They call them films, the rest of the world calls them adverts, puffs, promos. The nearest they get to real movie production is product placement. The nearest they get to being broadcast is when Channel 4 does a documentary on the industry. And even then they hit the cutting room floor.

Not Lilith's kind of place. Nevertheless, she finds herself swinging from a fire ladder high above the Soho roofscape at three in the morning softly intoning harmonies from early Cocteau Twins songs and she has to admit it has something going for it.

Someone two flights below is yelling at her to come down, which is taking the piss a bit since he gave her the drugs in the first place. She's watching the procession of faces in the clouds, waiting for André's. She knows it'll come because it does every time. Not a night has passed on E without his face appearing to her, whether out of the clouds, the trees or just the air itself. She knows all she has to do is touch it once and he will be banished for good.

She takes another step up the ladder. There's another wall about 15 feet up, another bit of roof. Renewed shouting from down below. Rising levels of hysteria sweeping up from the well of sound that is the party. Strange 80s disco tracks have replaced the hip hop and scratch beats since the DJ fucked off home a couple of hours ago.

All she has to do, to create the geomancer's 'city of fusion' and harmonise the landscape, is bring together the energies of earth and sky. She reaches for the clouds. That would do it.

Then she'd be free of him for ever.

Yeah.

Right.

1

Soho at five in the morning rivals pre-Revolution Bucharest as the most charmless place on the planet. Forget all this crap about café society, post-club cappuccino at Bar Italia – if Soho at dawn is a hub of anything, it's a hub of quiet despair. Taxis prowl like black panthers and all the poor, lost gazelle dreams of is to be eaten up by one. Money or no money. Every cabbie knows if he picks up a fare at first light in Soho he'll either be trekking round Forest Hill half an hour later looking for a cashpoint, some hopeless drunk in the back slurring the name of his bank, or sitting with the engine running, the *Sun* resting on the steering wheel and the meter ticking over outside some desolate East Finchley conversion, a young girl crashed out on an unmade bed two flights up.

Lilith flagged one down on Oxford Street. It looped around a traffic island, yellow bollards viciously bright in the limpid, post-dawn fumes. 'Shepherd's Bush,' she says as she climbs in the back, careful, even in the state she's in, not to give the driver the option. The number of times she's been stiffed trying to get back to Tottenham... Shepherd's Bush is closer but the thing to remember is that eight out of ten black-cab drivers are bastards.

She passes out, coming to miraculously just as they hit Holland Park roundabout – she likes its giant barometer, filled with gushing blue like a hypodermic, always has to give it the onceover whenever she comes this way. To ignore it would be to court disaster.

'Abdale Road,' she says once, distinctly, through the glass partition when he asks. 'Opposite the end of Ellerslie Road, you know.'

He grunts.

Yeah. Ignorant fuck.

The look he gives her when she counts out the right money and smiles her sweet smile, she can use that look. Store its malevolence and use it against him in the future. Him and his kind.

She waits till he's gone before pushing open the gate and dragging herself up the path to the front door. No point making it easy for him. Upstairs, she stands at the window staring up Ellerslie Road. Nothing. The sky holds no clues.

Overcast as far as she can see.

She collapses onto the mattress without taking her things off.

If she dreams she remembers nothing when she wakes at midday, her legs aching. As she fights to untie her Caterpillars she notices light blue scuff marks all over the toes and heels. She wets her finger and rubs at one or two but they just won't budge. She pushes her hair out of her face and thinks about the night before – vague memories of tearing up fire escapes, climbing up to the sky. Did she perhaps reach it? Is that it?

The flat is quiet, the other tenants out at work. She won this room on the toss of a coin. It's the biggest and has the best view – the break in the houses opposite to allow for Ellerslie Road gives good sunset – but she can't shake off its few ghosts. Something or someone still pollutes the atmosphere. The rancid smell of ancient couplings occasionally wakes her in the night. Not just one couple either. The room is a psychic bulletin board covered with old notices. As soon as she hits the mark with one or two decent magazines she'll be out of there and heading south of the Uxbridge Road. Not necessarily Brackenbury fucking Village, but definitely out of flame-throwing distance of the White City Estate.

In the pocket of her Helmut Lang jacket there's a handful of earth. She fishes it out and carries it to the kitchen where the floor is cleanest. Standing in the centre of the room, she opens her fist and allows the loose soil to tumble on to the off-white lino. Then she's down on her hands and knees looking for the lines. The lines that join the dots. She's looking for the pattern of the days. She's heard it called prophecy. This girl, this stylist, this... *geomancer*.

This time she doesn't look any of them in the eye. Not until she gets upstairs. Once again eight floors to check out her reflection. As if she doesn't already know it inside out.

'Hi,' she says to Jim Cover as she sashays – there's no other word for it – out of the lift.

He's already got a fag in his mouth this time. Does he recognise her? She can't tell.

'I came a couple of weeks ago,' she says, without losing any ground. 'You said you wanted to see some more.' She's really going for it. He's nodding, going, 'Yeah, yeah.' They sit. She slides the book across to him, sits back this time, crosses her legs. She's confident. Never been more so.

He starts quickly and has to go back, or slow down at least. She watches his thumb drift to the corner of the plastified page ready to turn it, then drop back: he keeps finding more stuff to look at – and he's looking at it *properly*. He's nodding now, making little grunting noises somewhere inside his oesophagus – he likes this stuff. Engrossed, he forgets that his cigarette is Bogarting between his fingers. Ash topples to the floor. He drops the butt absent-mindedly, nodding again. Reaches for another fag, lights it on autopilot.

'This is good,' he mumbles through constrained lips. 'You've, I dunno...

you've got...'

She doesn't need him to say it. She's knows she's got it this time. He's going to commission her to do something. He's not going to buy *these* pix – that's not the way it works – but he's going to buy some new stuff off of her. And he's going to pay her for it upfront.

And it was all from the lines. The dots and lines. The random dots of earth and the lines drawn between them.

She thinks back to her themed shoots. And everyone else's themed shoots. Desert islands, villas on the outskirts of Havana, unshaven guys with greasy hair and drooping braces, *Batman* pastiches, *Blade Runner* rip-offs, fake 40s postwar chic, stuff, stuff – stuff, stuff, stuff. She's left all that behind. Themes are out – the earth scattered on the kitchen floor told her – and random is in.

With this shoot she's gone against all fashion's received wisdom. She's used a thin, wasted-looking girl – so far so traditional – that she found loitering outside Boss Models in Berners Mews hoping to get spotted, and she's dressed her in a wild mish-mash of clashing styles. She's got her in a lilac suede shirtdress by Scooter, wedge-heeled black satin shoes from Prada, chain belt by Sally Gissing from Harvey Nichols and a black visor from Fabris Lane Etalia Sport. All of that lot photographed down a meagre cobbled alley off the Whitechapel Road.

Then she's taken her over to the DLR at Westferry and thrown at her a Nic Janik rayon-mix dress, brown-tinted goggles by Killer Loop and a pair of Christian Louboutin's fuchsia satin sling-backs. Wonderful disorder, horrible carnage. And Jim Cover's shaking his head, transported – as far as someone like him can be.

'This is... you know...'

She knows.

She smiles, crosses her legs like a man, catches sight of her boots – the blue scuff marks still there from the other night. The sign that she was going to make it sooner rather than later.

Little bits of sky.

Yeah, right.

BLUES IN THE BOTTLE

kirk lake

You've all had them I guess. Me, I've had a whole string of them and I'm not at the end of the rope yet.

I took a job at a dairy warehouse. A huge hangar full of UHT milk, long-life yoghurt and plastic wrapped cheese.

Summer mornings at 7.30 and the stench of curdled milk from split cases would hang in the air and seep into my nostrils churning my stomach before I'd even made it through the gates.

A buzz of flies, past dead rats and mice by the skip that all the broken stuff was hurled into.

I'd pick up the first roll of computer print-out that carried the order for some supermarket or other: 200 litres of red top UHT, 140 green, 50 blue, on and on... Wrapping and stacking onto pallets for 2.40 an hour, and this isn't so long ago that 2.40 meant shit.

The work was hard and heavy and the wrapping off the cartons and bottles would slice into your hands. Good, deep plastic cuts. Sharp as a Stanley into your fingers and palms, as you tried to split the cases, stacking up the right amount of stuff onto your pallet. Relentless. The computer spewed out order after order. They had a good crew working for them. Good for the work. The living dead. The breaks dragged longer than the shifts. They would talk about nothing and grab their dicks and shout "Get down and smoke that!" through the window whenever one of the younger secretaries walked past.

The guys that ran the forklifts were the worst. Running around the place, sat up there, smoking cigarettes thinking they were hot shit, like a throne on wheels. Mr Forklift King of stinking Milkdom. You had to deal with them though. When your order asked for something that you couldn't reach, you had to call on the forkers and they'd shrug and say "yeah, yeah, I'll get it when I'm ready".

I needed a crate of stuff brought down from the top shelf. Last item on the last order before lunch. I called over this driver. One of the worst. A flabby red-haired cunt that had called me a fucking queer

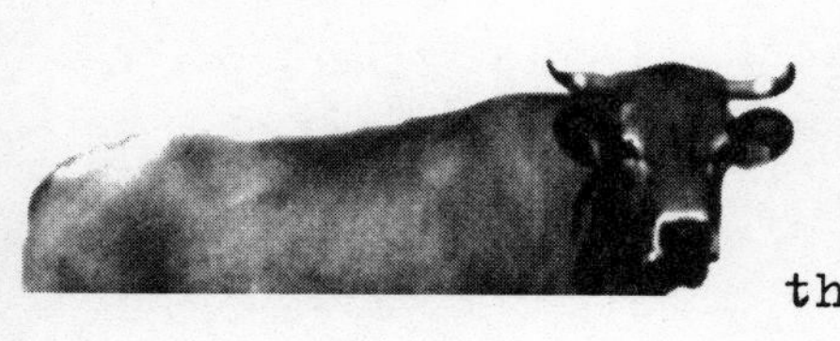

in a stage whisper because I hadn't shouted at any women at all even though I'd been there a couple of months.

He manoeuvred the fork and started digging out this pallet of long-life yoghurts from the top of the rack and the pallet slipped and caught at a 45° angle on the rack. The wood jammed so it wouldn't move one way or the other. King Fork had fucked up. He stepped down from the truck and walked over to me.

"Listen kid," he said, "why don't you climb up there and loosen it up so I can get a bite at it with the forks?" He pointed up to the ceiling, way up there.

I shrugged my shoulders. "Uhh, I don't think so. I can't finish this order until you get that thing down, and I'm not going up there, so I guess you're going to have to do it yourself."

I looked up at the yoghurt swelling against the plastic wrap, then put my order in my overalls pocket and started walking to the locker-room.

He jumped back in the forklift, called me an arrogant fucker and started it up. Pulled it back a little then rammed in the forks so it caught on the wood at the bottom of the pallet. Then in and out, up and down. Going at it like a dog at a tree swing tyre, until I heard the wood crack and the plastic creak and watched the pallet slip

d o w n between the racks and the whole tower of y o g h u r t come crashing down onto the grilled cover of the forklift.

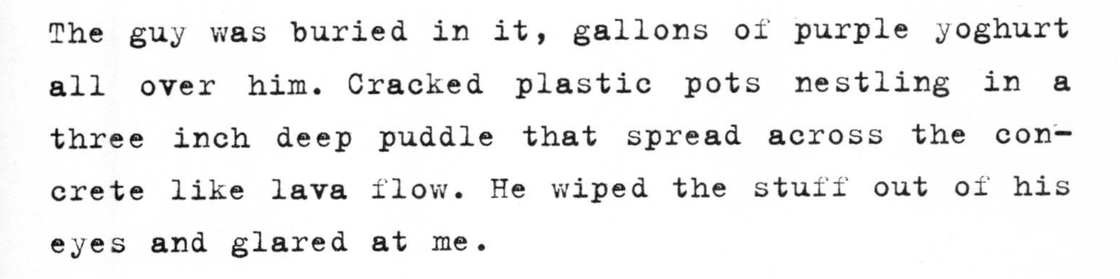

The guy was buried in it, gallons of purple yoghurt all over him. Cracked plastic pots nestling in a three inch deep puddle that spread across the concrete like lava flow. He wiped the stuff out of his eyes and glared at me.

The foreman came running over and told me to go fetch a broom and shovel. King Fork jumped from his truck dripping yoghurt like a mauve melting man. I walked over to the place where they kept the cleaning stuff and kept on walking. Got my things from my locker and kept walking right out of the gate. Even the milk-sick air smelled sweet.

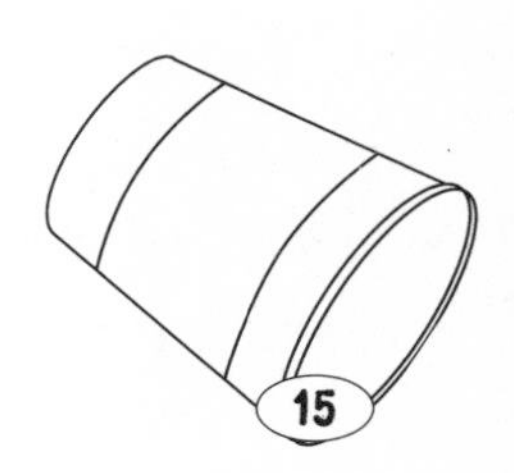

stationary

SONYA AURORA MADAN - ECHOBELLY

Stood up at the border station
Used up all my sodding patience
Offered all to soul salvation
Sandwich choice of God and nation
Haloed voice, chiselled faces
Fill your head with empty spaces

Once again a leader nation
Pay the price of approbation
Weeding out for information
Choke the cheers with punctuation
Lead us into sweet temptation

Glory to the new dictator
Power - drug - initiator
Mothers dressed in alligator
All good children love to hate her

Make it on the elevator
Shove it in a liquidator

Twisted heart - body blitzed
Screw it tight and make it fit
Can't be felt until you kick
Make you laugh - you make me sick
Nothing but a little prick.

pecan  pie

Sarah Jane

Heather opened the front door, to be greeted by a sunburnt smiling face.

"I've brought you pecan pie, and chocolate milk and a fresh carton of your favourite cancer sticks. It's *so* good to see you again... I *know* it was only yesterday, but, well, it sure gets lonesome in those city scrapers they call tower-blocks."

Heather smiled, attempting to laugh at Annie's camp sense of humour, but ended up in tears. Annie dropped the groceries, and hugged her.

"I have to go," explained Heather. "Ed's father has been stabbed or wounded or... something... I don't know. He's in the hospital and I have to go meet Ed right now. I don't understand, what can I do? I'm meant to be entertaining Thom. Shit."

Heather's head dropped onto Annie's shoulder, her shakes vibrating through both of them.

Annie tried to act confident. "Look H, you go. I'll stay here and look after Thom. You need a cab or anything?"

Heather tried to collect herself and scrambled around on the floor, looking for a bunch of keys. She reached underneath a bowl of dried cereal and pulled out a Gladiators key-ring.

"Okay. I'll call you later. If Ed phones..."

Annie gave Heather one last hug and guided her onto the pavement. The pecan pie and the milk, and the now crushed cancer sticks are all still lying in the doorway. Annie waved Heather off, then turned around to pick up the groceries. Murder. Violence. Stabbings. Ed's father. Holy shit.

Annie strolled towards the kitchen, cradling the groceries. Acres of dirty pots, smashed glasses, and twisted cutlery littered the room. The cupboards were virtually empty but for dust, and the fridge door was wide open.

"Hi, what are you up to?"

A voice from the doorway echoed through the room. It belonged to Thom, Heather's baby brother. I say baby, but really Thom is seventeen and extremely streetwise. He just *looks* young.

Annie smiled. "You want some pie, Thom?"

"Maybe."

Thom leaned against the wall, his eyes tracing the outline of Annie's body. Immediately, he notices the keys (hanging from the corner of Annie's leather) and starts fantasizing about what they may or may not open. He's not altogether certain, but he figures they may be for a pair of handcuffs, since George has a similar key. George is a notorious masochist, and Thom's on-and-off best friend.

"You work in a comic store, don't you?"

"Yeah," replied Annie. "A nine to five surrounded by Superman, Wonder Woman, The Joker, Death, and *lots* of teenage *freaks*."

Annie emphasised the word "freaks" in a chilly gothic voice, and tried not too grin too much. Thom was quite charming for an adolescent, and though he looked skinny, he was probably ten or eleven stone. His mouth was lovely, lush full lips the colour of blood; but his eyes let him down, they were a blank, easily forgettable, washed out shade of blue.

Never mind, thought Annie, he's still pretty adorable. I could play around with him. Heather wouldn't mind *that* much, or she needn't find out, I mean...

"How old are you?"

"Twenty one," Annie lied. "Enough questions, pour us some milk. We'll go listen to a record, watch a movie, crash out, or something..."

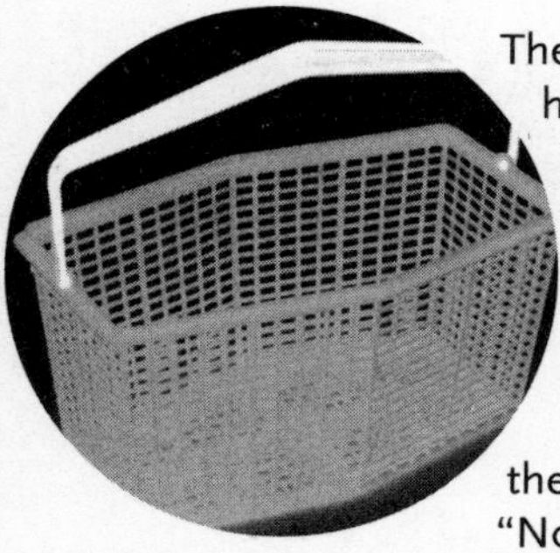

The "something" lingered in the air all afternoon, and three hours later Annie and Thom are still sitting in the lounge/convertible bedroom, discussing religion, sex, death, and murder. (Well, in all honesty, religion was abandoned pretty quickly since both Thom and Annie are headstrong atheists, but the rest of the conversation was, well, fairly coherent.)

"I know what I am," Thom chuckles. "I'm a pagan, a heathen, an unbeliever."

"No, you're not," Annie protests, with a deliciously devilish smile. "You're... a reprobate, a social outcast, a celestial Beelzebub."

Thom's face boasts a curious smile. "You are trying to conjure and bewitch me. Admit it. You want to exorcise spirits from me. I've met you before, in another body, another century. You're a vampire, aren't you? Well, don't you worry, I could out voodoo you any day."

Annie laughs perhaps a little too heartily. "Seriously my dear Lucifer, what interests you?"

"What interests me," Thom replies, after a long pregnant pause, "is what happens *after* the last boat or the last tube leaves. Just *supposing* you miss it, either deliberately or accidentally, what happens then? Let's suppose I missed the plane back from L.A." (Thom has been in L.A. for the last half a year, visiting his and Heather's alcoholic mother, Diane. Diane was a big soap star in the late seventies and is now struggling to cope with the reality of her life.)

"Suppose I was there at the airport, *stranded*, with no money or food: *nothing*. What would I do?"

Thom's face widens, showing gleaming white teeth. He looks... kind of... possessed? "Desperation, that's *exactly* what interests me. People living by their wits, willing to take a few risks, juggle with death even."

He stops to grab a spoonful of pie, and turns up the stereo. Music plays loudly, meaning neither Thom nor Annie can completely work out what the other is saying. A spiral of guitars, then a melancholic Billy Corgan fills the room. Annie hums a little, recognising the song, something about being killed, or killing.

"What happens in the darkness, is of *pleasure* and *anxiety* to us all." Thom adopts the voice of a gothic narrator. "How many films and books have been devoted to the darkness, to evil spirits, illicit sex, murder even?" He smiles sadistically. "There's hundreds of horror films alone, and why do we watch them? Are we merely voyeurs, too shit scared to act on our impulses? We are, aren't we? We're little more than cultivated animals, savages, libertines."

Annie grins, thinking that Thom is rather delicious in a geekish kind of way. If only he'd stop waffling on about horror, existentialism, nihilism, death, for just an hour or two, he would probably get laid a lot more. Especially, and at this thought Annie smirks, because not only is he young and naive looking, but he's blond. He's like a blow-up Hollywood TV star, thinks Annie, only instead of quoting movies, he quotes Baudelaire and Camus, and all that romantic death shit.

"What are your impulses?" Thom interrupts.

Annie laughs nervously. "You want mine? What do you want exactly, my desires, my dreams, what?"

"What strikes you here (in the heart) and what excites you here!' Thom scratches his crotch. "Things that other people might consider, a little... perverse... sick... kinky. You know what I'm saying, I can tell you do... c'mon, open up."

Thom takes a step backwards to lean against something. He can't help noticing the beautiful bulge in Annie's jeans. It would be easy enough to just undo them and to grab at that sweet cock, to even engage Annie in a mutual jerking off, but Thom wants something more. Something not necessarily spiritual, but something a little strange, dangerous, or wrong.

Thom looks across the room, Annie is peering down at his Adidas like they're going to help him talk. He looks... what? Half embarrassed, half pleased? Annie coughs slightly, and then sits up straight, his eyes piercing Thom's bemused and excited face.

"I want... to fuck you."

Thom's face appears momentarily blank, like he's heard the news of an accident or fatality.

Annie continues." I want to rip those shorts off that superior ass of yours and to bury my head in your crotch." He moves closer to Thom, stopping a small footstep away, then kneels down, lightly brushing his lips against the fly of Thom's pants. He smiles, feeling the outline of a solid erect cock.

"I want to let you ride the corners of my mouth... and then, I want you to beg me to let you come. I won't agree immediately of course, but eventually..." He kisses Thom's jean-shorts again, only this time, making sure he presses hard enough to create a little friction. "Then... I'd want a hot bath, and a large cold... beer!" He grins at the shining face above him. "If you were very lucky, and I mean very, I'd lubricate this magnificent cock of mine and I'd fit it into your tight baby asshole."

Thom moans slightly, his usually beyond white face boasting a pale pink shade. His hands look awkward, and he thinks about placing them on Annie's shoulders. Would that be too forward? Or too clumsy?

"What else?" he asks Annie quietly.

"I'd wait... until you were about to come... about to love the feel of me, snug up inside you, and then... I'd kill you."

Annie smiles to himself. He doesn't mean a word of it, he's just saying what he thinks Thom longs to hear. He does want to sleep with Thom, maybe, but the shit he's just spouted had nothing to do with him. Those weren't his impulses, his desires or his dreams, nor even his nightmares: they were the words of a throwaway porn film. Annie himself could never construct such sentences. He looks over at Thom, and for a moment or two, the air is penetrated with silence.

"You're a prince," Thom whispers. "You are..." He chokes on his words, unable to speak, and Annie witnesses what he thinks is a tear roll slowly down Thom's left cheek.

It's so pathetic Annie almost laughs. Thom is obviously so crazed and so fucked up that he *wants* to die in the hands of a stranger. Okay, he thinks, I'm not a stranger, but almost. Annie despairs: What if Thom *does* meet some loon? Somebody who would grant him his wish. Fuck it, he feels sick at the very prospect of it. Okay, he tells himself, Thom is kinda sincere, kinda romantic, but this stupid subversive death wish? Annie closes his eyes. He once read an interesting essay on "The Sublime and the Beautiful", but he found it too difficult to make sense of. Maybe this is what obsesses Thom, some weird idea of working towards an enlightenment? Annie shrugs his shoulders. A body is just skin and bones, isn't it?

"Save me. Save me... from myself. You're a God, an angel, a saint." Thom's face glistens in the light. "I... I almost love you. You are... SO fucking beautiful."

Annie blushes, but has no idea why. He doesn't feel flattered or worthy, or anything. He looks at the poster concealed by Thom, and manages to decipher the image of A Clockwork Orange. Neat poster, he thinks, but now what?

"Annie, Ann... you want... to have some sex? I got some rubbers, and some lube, in that case over there."

Thom points to a bag in the middle of the room and lies down on the floor. He selects a new tape and feeds it into the battered stereo. A fast electronic sound rushes through the room. The music is all keyboards, samples and high pitched squeals. Bastard techno, thinks Thom, I *hate* this shit, whose tape is it? Annie thinks the same, but neither of them speak. He looks at Thom, balancing in-between record sleeves and ashtrays.

The words "I almost love you" flicker through his head, then disappear.

ELASTIC ETHER

ROBIN RIMBAUD / SCANNER

What are you up to then? oh I've just come in, thought I'd

alright…you didn't go screwing around with girls

watch a couple of movies, see what's on the old

different girl every night,did you? You didn't go

movie channel **yeah, you been working hard?** no!

just jumping into bed with'em and that's it…that's

I've just had a nice easy day today… I got invited to a ball

what he does, innit? he hasn't had a steady girlfriend for

on the 24th of October **a ball! ooh, that sounds nice** I know,

ages, you think he's about to want one now and do you think

it sounds pretty good, so I think I'll go to that, and a friend

I'm about to wanna a steady boyfriend again…nah…no thank

of mine said they could get me some tickets to a couple of

you no no I'm not having no sexual thing with michael,

concerts coming up **what kind of concerts are they?**

tony, right, because he's slept with so many girls yeah, he just…it doesn't mean nothing to him so I wouldn't sleep with

er… en vogue **that sounds nice, yeah…** oh, I haven't seen you

michael - he's just a friend,that is all…that is all he is,

yet have I? **that's true** the truth is, I don't know

and that's all I want it to stay as well; if I go with him,

whether you're attractive and stuff **oh I am,**

I go with him, but it ain't gonna mean nothing to me more than

you won't be disappointed, I told you that

just friends… me and you used to go out as friends and nothing

in the beginning didn't I? yeah I know, but you

happened did it?…did it?…tony?…well then… you're in bed now

could have just been saying that **no, I'm not saying that**

int ya? huh huh… well then, ya know what I mean, so nothing

everyone says I'm attractive, my eyes are captive…and my

has to happen between me and michael, and nothing has to happen

figure and my bubbling personality what sort of a

between you and that girl if you don't want it to, so it ain't

figure do you have? **24 waist** oh wow, so you're pretty

about to...the way I'm going on is that it will happen between you

slim are you? ...you tallish? **yeah, I'm 5 foot 7**

and that girl because I never had specifically gave michael my

you're joking! **no I'm not, 5 foot 7, 24-inch waist,**

telephone number right and that he never gave me his, especially

36B bust, so I'm busty oh really! **medium short black hair,**

as you gave her your mobile number...you spoke to her a couple of

I've got a nice tan are you pretty sexy? **yeah, you ought to**

nights ago right...I mean it's not as if it's a one-off thing...

see the clothes I wear! huh! what sort of things do you wear?

oh right! we'll arrange to go out for a friendly drink next week

nice sorta stuff, hee hee, you won't be disappointed

and that's it, you don't talk to each other until then right,

if you see me anyway alright what do you have that's

it's not like that, you're talking to her throughout the week and

really daring? **oh, I've got a short black mini**

you're more likely to phone her tomorrow or whenever...and

skirt right and I've got stockings and high heels,

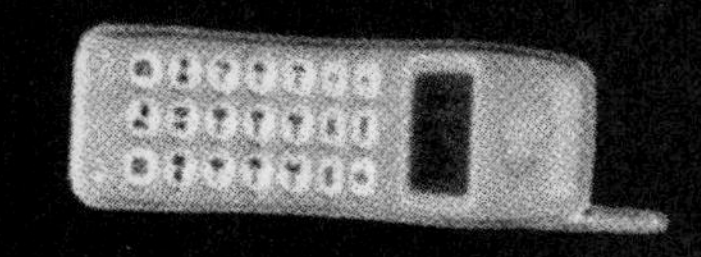

then...no...yeah, you know, I ain't changed the way, I ain't changed

I've got all sorts of things really? what do you have that's

my opinion or nothing...I still don't wanna get involved with

really rude and daring? **oh, I don't know whether I've got**

no-one else...that don't mean I can't have friends...don't you agree

my nurses uniform, hang on, I'll just have a look...

with me?...eh?...you do?...do you agree with me?...you see, why phone

I'm just having a look through my drawer at the

and not listen?...I wanna talk to you about this...alright? then I'll

moment shall I tell you what I have in my

go, right...anyway what was I saying? we won't talk to each other

drawer?...suspender belts, shirts, hot pants, bras, knickers

for a while right, that's what you want and it'll give you time

have you...have you got anything that's really rude and short?

to sort out, you know what I mean?...uh...alright, we won't talk to

yeah my black skirt is really, really short is it? **yeah,**

each other ever again will that be better? cut each other

really really short you know like school skirts,

completely off...would that be better? look tony, you're the one

st trinians? **something like that but it's just really**

making the decisions yeah?... so how long don't ya wanna talk to

short and tight oh right, let's go for it! **you know how much**

each other for? a month? a couple of weeks? it's up to you... we

it is don't you? yeah...oh right, you said you only stay for

don't have to talk to each other ever again, if that's what you

an hour **well, yeah, you'll have a good time anyway, you'd**

really want, that's how it's gonna be, I just wannna sort it out

be too tired, too tired by the time I've finished with you.

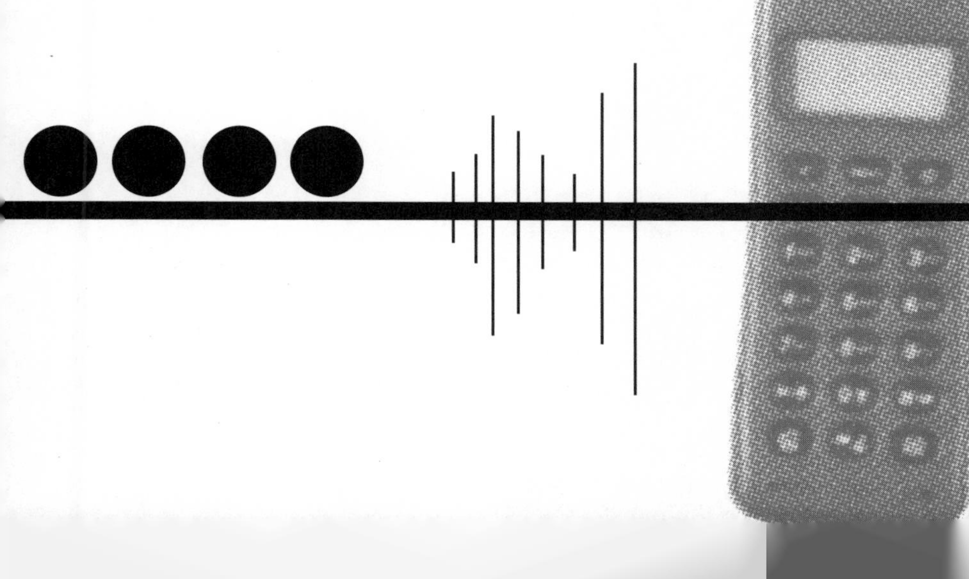

selling sweatshirts on venice beach

Liz driving, Troy in the back,
I'm on the roof rack,
behaving like Jack.
Heading into the mystic.
Venice Beach.
I thought this only existed in worn out beat books.

The sun warm;
my mind and heart flying like a mosquitto on amphetamines,
cars, girls, flags and mountains.
I'm freeway freeloading as if I may go blind at any moment.

Venice Beach is a Californian bazaar,
bizarre to the extreme.
Cats on skateboards selling surfing caps.
Latino lovers selling cheap sunglasses.
New-Age neurotics selling nothing but bad jokes.
Music, lights and colour.

A voice from the assembled babes in toyland.
"Sweatshirts, two for twenty five dollars. I'm giving them away mate."
"Where are you from?" I ask shaking.
"Hackney."
"What are you doing here?"
"Selling sweatshirts you stupid prat!"
I smile like a facial slash victim.

My national pride is a personal pride.
I hope you understand.

ralph dartford

repeater

STEVE AYLETT

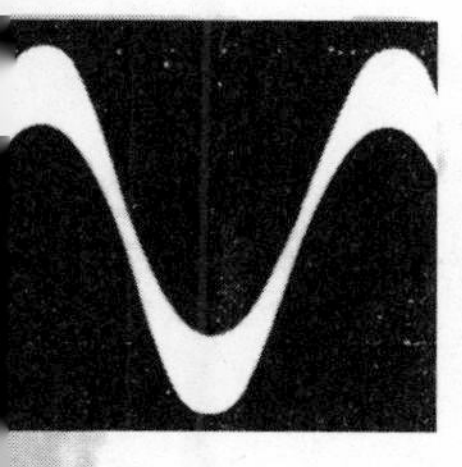

After an hour recording parkbirds I strolled back through town, the mike in my shoulderbag laying down the traffic. Streets like the deeps of a full ashtray. A plaingarb cop trundled up offering drugs. I declined and was arrested. At the kennel the cops were embarrassed and angry when I replayed the proof of my lamblike innocence. As they handed me my jaw on a plate, I had an idea. Saw it all red and gold and full of justice. Put it at the front of a piece of Debussy and let the music carry it forward, filling it out. A notion and a half. Have to ask the old soldier.

The beating was over and I hadn't noticed. Cops regarding me with stall-cod eyes. Time to get up – but don't do it again.

Back on the street feeling four snapped ribs – I've had worse and laughed with the correct medication. It was partly my fault for taking that route. The area was famous for the cops' planting of drugs and users had begun flocking there in the hope of being able to keep some in exchange for violence. But I wondered what Dogger would say.

The old soldier lived in a shed apparently made of biscuit and was never without his dog Fire, the calling of whose name caused alarm and mayhem. Dogger had dodged so many bad laws his spine had corkscrewed. In classic style he had swallowed media promises of a better life and then overstepped the boundary of etiquette by actually trying to secure one. He was like Fagin without the charm and carried lemons in his coat as a teargas precaution. He was so real his toaster ran on diesel. As I descended the railway embankment I heard him yelling in the hut. 'The chains of your repression are as familiar to you as the teeth in your head. Born to it you were.'

'Hello Dogger,' I said cautiously, entering. He was alone. I told him about the cops' theft of my equipment.

'There's no limit to what a dying system will demand of you, Hypnojerry,' he laughed, showing braces like a knuckleduster. 'Only a narrow land could end at one stroke the right to sound and the right to silence.' He was referring to a brace of new laws which curtailed the activities of those with an aptitude for reflection and enjoyment. 'For fear of copycat outbreaks of happiness and laughter. Not that the deeper implications matter to a public soundproofed by indifference. Sad as a galleon in a bottle.'

His hands flew over the eight-track sound desk. He was messing with the sound of a prefab saying 'nothing you need fear' – it was reversed, accelerated, cracked like a whip. 'They did the same to me – tried to send me to clench for Heseltine possession.' This was a laugh as cocaine will have slowed Dogger's thoughts to a constabulary crawl. He had an eight-track mind. 'It's genius envy, Jell, pure and sour. I felt pity for the bastards so as not to get too angry. Injustice rings down through history to a deserted callbox. Let stress get into your tripes, you'll end up in surgery under a blithe knife. Watch this.' And he played the word 'fear' while pointing to a screen where the sound was rendered as a geometrical netshape which bulbed like a soapbubble. He tapped at a keyboard which froze the shape, then flipped it inside-out like a mitten. 'Now let's play this shape as a noise,' he said, and pressed return. The system emitted the worst fart I'd ever heard.

Dogger explained that he had found a way to disclose the inner nature of a recorded verbal statement. Some remarks produced the zenlike sound of a gong. Others – particularly those of the young – the howl of a desert wind. Politicians from both Dum and Dee almost always created flatulence.

It was the latest in a long course of experimentation. Dogger had discovered birdsong slowed down was whalenoise and whalenoise speeded up was birdsong. He found that Nixon's resignation speech reversed was an invocation to the Devil in exquisitely pronounced Lithuanian. When he heard about the rave laws outlawing repetitive beats he examined the issue in fly-leg detail. Rhythm requires an alternation between sound and silence, or between one sound and another. Dogger had considered whether the legislation could apply to repetitive injustice and bullshit but these activities were so constant as to be a seamless, mundane hum. Only regular interruptions of this mundanity could set up a beat. That was why raves were against the law – so that the unjust and dishonest would not be seen to be part of an illegal process. 'It's all in the game, Hypnojerry. Mischief distinguishes man from the other animals – that and the opposable thumb.'

A train shrieked past and Fire woke up, raising his ears and eyebrows.

The next evening we retrieved my gear with the help of Antifrog. We figured since two wrongs don't make a right, our act would not stand out against the general corruption. Antifrog was a gay black youth with a strong Irish accent and herbal trousers. When this montage of minorities swanned into the kennel the cops couldn't believe their luck and set about his punishment. Truncheons leapt like salmon as he tried to report a theft. Dogger and I slipped past before the party was dampened by blood and boredom.

Since the passing of the new laws so much sound equipment had been seized we had learned that the safest thing to do was break into the cop confiscation store and dump our stuff there without a tag. Other than drugs they never touched a thing. But with the party approaching we'd need the gear and for once we had a legitimate reason for entry – my recording rig. Dogger kept up a running commentary as he worked the bolt cutters – he'd speak till the bitter, amp-smashing end. 'Almost gave up on your generation, Jell. Tunnel vision without a flashlight. A passionless blank. Then by god the colour started seeping out of the walls. Back from the dead – and me too. Should have seen me in the eighties, boy – so out of it I had sideburns on someone else's face. Then one day I strode toward the horizon and was damn near garrotted by a rainbow.'

We were into the storeroom – I found my equipment and knew this was the only way I could have retrieved it. The truth is easiest to disprove. Its defences are down.

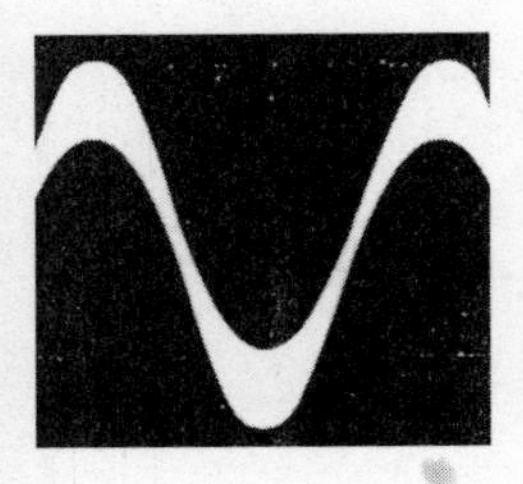

Dogger meanwhile was flashing a Mysteron beam over amplifier stacks – the stuff of villainy. 'Jell, disorder's an offence with no mappable contours and the ideal fog for all occasions. Laws have gone by like motes on the film of my eye and with as much effect – but disorder? By god it's a beauty.'

'We're in a hurry-up,' I took the precaution of reminding him.

But Dogger had a philosophy you could stand a spoon in – he took a book from a shelf, blowing at the dust and frowning. '*After London*. Damn fine book – you can keep your triffids. Jefferies got there first, with a flood. Well written too.'

'Most books are so well written they barely have any effect on the reader's senses,' I told him urgently. 'Let's conclude this procedure and get out.'

'With a bang or a whimper though Jell, how'd you picture it ending? The world, I mean?' We lifted the stack amp between us and started off. 'Here's how I see it,' Dogger grunted through his exertions. 'Denial. Vacuum competes with vacuum. Laws outlaw the harmless to make the effective inconceivable. Scholarly incomprehension. No questions asked. Banality given the terms and prestige of science. Ignorance worn like a heraldic crest. Mediocrity loudly rewarded. Misery by instalments. Hypocrisy too extreme to process. Maintenance of a feeble public imagination. Lavish access to useless data. Fashion as misdirection. Social meltdown in a cascade pattern, consumed by a drought of significance. Drabness as ordered as the grey cells of a deserted waspnest.'

'It's a thought.'

On the way out we were approached by someone as featureless as a figure in a crash procedure diagram. It asked who we were and we pretended to be cops by saying we didn't know.

A few days later we visited Antifrog in hospital. The beating had been worse than we expected but he wished us well through a broken mouth. We taped the irregular bleep of his coronary monitor and set off for the country. A convoy of cars processioned through darkness toward a repeated thumping which could have been the heartbeat of the land itself. By degrees it became audible as Ravel's *Bolero*, played across a fallow field stretching so far it seemed not to end. Acres of grass were blown to italics. Fire leapt from the van and started across the field, eager for fun.

By midnight the field was a sea of ethnic trousers and Evian bottles. I remember weird strobe images of Dogger looking as spooky as a pickled alien. Lasers of jade and red gold were fanning and dipping as Antifrog's heartrate formed the grid for a soundscape sampled from the net and forced through a 50,000 watt sound system. In the crowd it was hard to tell where one smile ended and another began. Without lying there was nothing bad to be said about it. The press would have a field day.

Dogger and I had wired ourselves and some others with cop-style bodymikes which relayed crowdnoise through an oscillating sampler. Dogger disappeared but I heard him talking again, taking full advantage of the mike – rantbites were firing off and jarring with the ambience. 'Cancering anxiety. Sneering at tradition. A government openly at war with its people. Why be covert in the last ditch?' I waded through the scene to strangle him – no polemics, Dogger, not *now*.

I saw blurlights playing over a marquee wall and wondered how a set of old pub strobes had got in here. A repetitive siren effect was cranked up in the mix – *this sound is illegal*, I thought vaguely, and passing outside found it was caused by countless police cars surrounding the area. Blue lights strobed in the night.

The cops stood expecting our amusement to be paralysed in deference. Many had confused their profession with full human identity. I thought a few had guns, and asked someone why.

'To assure us that nice people use guns too.'

One cop was yelling inaudibly through a loudhailer. I learned later that this official warning to leave was a mere formality, but as the cop put the hailer aside and signalled the others to move in, a loop of his statement volleyed from the speakerstacks. Most of the ravers took it as a joke, but a thousand wandered out and the cops, finding they had lost the element of surprise, panicked.

Looking back I can see that all the components of hell were assembled. The cops terrified the crowd in an ironic and post-modern attempt to provoke order. A few less educated ravers didn't get the reference and became angry. These signals were elaborately ignored and the order to move on repeated. Again someone's mike picked up the message and rendered it audible, increasing the crowd outside the main marquee. The cops said that failure to comply would be considered an act of aggression. Dizzy with the notion that a thing could be considered something it wasn't, the crowd yelled back that cop helmets would be considered anchovies and that the cops themselves were chimps in cashmere. There was a cold explosion.

Add velocity to ignorance and you get a police car. One sped into the crowd and screeched to a halt as a girl twisted through the air and landed in a heap. A new sound spat out of the speakers – a crack and then a squelch, like someone treading on a snail. Near the cop ranks someone's head had been rolled over – grey brain tangled with grey hair.

It was Dogger.

Amid the sequencers and scenes of riot several wired subjects were beaten repeatedly, each blow being re-broadcast from the rave stacks. A mile away, plaster ducks fell from cottage walls as the sound of a skull being struck repeatedly echoed through the early hours. The regular succession of blows made looping redundant. The rhythm of three different beatings merged and intersected like a multitracking beatbox, the occasional bone-snap an added punctuation. Rather than look vigilantly the other way, senior officers drove the mayhem. Blood dark as spilled petrol flared pillar-box red in the streak of torchbeams. Windscreens spiderwebbed, smoke drifted and the volume increased as shadowy figures became meaningless smudges of chaotic movement. Shots were followed by screams. It was like an Italian wedding.

A cold sun rose over the ghost of a good time. A few survivors wandered dazed. Picking through a dawn of Chaplin grey, I wished Dogger was alive or wrong. But he was neither and his passing was a deadbolt on any objective reflection. As far as I was concerned there had once been giants in the earth and now there was only plastic. Truth withered on the vine as the raid was declared a victory for common sense. Four deaths not including Dogger, who didn't count because he was old, and twelve others who didn't count because they weren't cops either. It was clarified that repetitive beating of a live skull in the course of police duty was legal but that acoustic amplification of the sound was not. The rave organisers, who had hired the land, decided to save money by trespassing for the next event.

I had Fire to look after. This charge looked to me in expectation of something I couldn't guess. Finally he decided I wasn't Dogger and wandered off. My generation lacked some essential element – I only hoped this made us unpredictable.

The authorities had taken action hoping some miracle would prevent an equal and opposite reaction, but no miracle materialised. Youth retaliation was swift and violent though sad beyond its years. Dogger had called us a dull bruise pounded over and over. A sleepy generation with the rave scene acting as a giant alarm. And he never would listen when I told him the weariness was understandable – for a brood overseen by those who make the same mistake and act surprised at the same result again and again and again and again and again and again and again.

Drive in

m dawes

Amongst the black, tangled mat of hair that wove through my fingers lay some flakes of skin and a small opaque smear of blood. The moment expanded out through a random scattering of timescales. Although I was looking at the aftermath of my impetuousness, I could still sense the warm, silken feeling of those live hairs as they lay across your head; and the rip, an accurate and sickening rip, as they left your scalp twined around my fingers. Before, during and after; the frozen expression in your face, your shoulders and knees hunched right up, the windscreen wipers squeaking a downstroke on the glass at exactly the wrong moment. A single instant, heavy with implications that would take hours to decipher, to decide whether to cry or laugh about. I hadn't the time to choose. From that point on there were instincts, chemicals, nervous signals in the spine, presumptions rising from the mind like vapours, guesses dropping through the chest like hot stones. Somewhere, a pragmatic and comforting instinct counted *1-2-3-4-5 screech 1-2-3-4-5 screech*, setting a schedule for my reactions to ensure they didn't coincide with the wiper blades. I wasn't surprised that you reacted first, I was surprised at how you reacted. Your kiss was gentle, but carried no sensation of forgiveness. It aroused me because I sensed that you wanted me more now than

you ever had since we met. It worried me because it was impossible to respond to.
The wipers whined again. From the speakers outside the window came the sound of wheels skidding on gravel as a big thirties car spun out of control on the screen ahead. ***Paper Moon,*** you'd said, ***one of the best. I'll back up.*** You reversed until the car sat in the lay-by, ticking over in front of the chipboard sign.

MOVIERAMA
Scotland's only Drive-In Movie !
Experience open-air wide-screen cinema
from the comfort of your own car

SHOWING TONIGHT 7PM
Road Movie Double Bill

PAPER MOON & EASY RIDER

100 yards on the right, 1 mile down track
Snacks and drinks available !

We'll go you said. I didn't argue and I didn't agree. We'd been driving since five in the morning. I wanted to hear a different sound to the suffocating hum of the engine, to be still instead of rocking and bumping and lurching over deserted roads.
We can talk you'd said. The night before we'd fought from seven until two, fell asleep at the table and dozed until the sun was almost up. I woke when a news bulletin came on television; I saw you hunched, rubbing your eyes, running your nails into your forearm, raising tracks on the skin. You dipped your fingers into a cup and flicked cold coffee at the newscaster, resentful at the fanfare music and the cultivated voice. When I switched off the TV and wiped the screen you snatched up the car keys and I knew that, uninvited, I was meant to follow you.
We only stopped twice in that whole day, once for petrol and once to fill the radiator. We didn't pay for the petrol, and as we watched the attendant run out of the garage in the mirrors, there was a momentary thaw between us, a sense of intimacy briefly restored by collusion in a small crime. But that didn't last long; the restrained smiles faded and the excitement died away, and the space between us filled up

once again with looming icebergs and impenetrable mist and the deafening drone of the engine.
In retrospect, I could see that your keenness to go to the drive-in stemmed from that solitary conversation during the drive. ***We can talk***, you'd said, deliberately taking off too fast and screaming to an abrupt halt at the lights on the corner of our street. We didn't talk. We crossed the border and came back again before we spoke. ***It's like a film*** you said, and not waiting for me to show myself curious, you went on, smiling faintly at the pleasure your ideas gave you. ***The way the sky and hills and signs pass by the windows, it's as if we were in a film and they were doing one of those back projections with a car being shaken by extras while they project a moving landscape outside the car.*** I knew what you were talking about but not why it was significant. ***All this,*** left hand lifting off the gearstick to gesture at outside, ***its like fucking television. It moves, it's in colour, it's behind glass,*** your voice becoming croaky and arched, ***and it doesn't make any fucking sense.*** I said ***Why don't you stop and get out?*** 
I was surprised when you didn't accelerate. Instead your expression softened a little and you checked the driving mirror a few times to maneuver tears away from your eyelids. I saw you pluck a random subject from thin air. ***I don't want to live in a city any more***, you said, ***but I can't come to the country. I can't look anywhere without needing a signal or a message to give it some sense. Doesn't matter if it's beautiful or not, I need words to read, I need people gesturing to each other, I need man-made things all around so that I'm not tempted to understand. Out here there's nothing to ridicule, nothing to get cynical about. I feel like I can accept it all. And that means accepting myself, and I'm not ready to do that. It never used to matter. I can't see all this. I feel like a camera, not a human being. I see something and congratulate myself for pinning it down and being able to interpret it. I'm not interested in it, it just drifts in and I give it a name and keep it. All this, its just flatness against this glass***, and you palmed the windscreen, ***or flatness up against my eyeballs, and I don't***

care how pretty it is, I want to be in it, not watching it. I asked ***Have you got your lenses in? Of course not,*** you sniffed.
I managed to stay awake the rest of the day by paying close attention to your movie as it swarmed over the surface of the car. It kept me quite engrossed because I could see no way of it coming to a rapid end. I followed it like a story in the hope that the successions of hills and rivers and junctions and parallel roadways would yield a plot. I waited for that fifteen-minutes-to-go feeling where the loose ends get conveniently and simultaneously tied up. Instead it all just ran out.
We were the second car at the drive-in and the only one occupied. Straight ahead was an appropriated billboard, painted white and speckled in birdshit. All around the site was a moor of scrubby grass and gorse bushes. Behind the car was a rickety, two storey structure like a stretched garden shed, with no lights on. The corrugated iron surface had a covered window at the top and a sign painted by the front door saying ***Snacks and Burgers.*** Beyond the building, the hillside fell away to the road below and further on to a small loch, faithfully reflecting a featureless grey sky turning dark. ***I've always wanted to go to a drive-in,*** I said, careful not to sound hollow with enthusiasm. ***It's the kind of thing people do in films. It's something I've always wanted to do for real.*** The same song must have entered both our heads at the same time. You sang a little, slowly and a bit flat. ***We've seen it in the movies, now let's see if it's true-ue-ue-ue.*** You leaned back, closing your eyes. I waited until I could be sure you were sleeping, then put my head in your lap and dozed, hoping I'd wake first.
I woke up to someone impatiently sounding their horn. You had lifted my t-shirt up and were carving lines into my back with your nails, which were short and stubby but sharp enough. There was no pattern, just a group of red weals, rising up and tingling like an itch. I stayed where I was and luxuriated in the feeling that at last you were touching me because you wanted to, not because you wanted to please me. After a few more impatient horn-blasts from outside, a light burst out of the opening in the shack and a picture flickered onto the screen. On my sleeve was a little ball of trapped fluff, which I chose to watch rather than the picture. Each time I exhaled from my nose, the

fluff shimmered in my breath like a flag. When you dug your nails in more deeply, the shock and the pleasure forced air more quickly out of me, making the fluff wave more frantically. You lifted my head and turned it forward. Through the windscreen and the streams of rain I could see a car driving along a straight, flat, American road, incapable of dodging the screen birdshit. I sat up and turned on the wipers. Eight other cars pointed themselves at the journey of flat moving lights caught on the screen.
We watched in silence for a minute, drowsily becoming engrossed in the image. Without turning to me, your arm swung around in front of you, your fist bouncing off my breastbone, a hollow thud like a slackened drumskin accompanying the feeling of my windpipe closing and my neck muscles jumping away in fright. Just as suddenly your hands changed function, pulling my head gently but swiftly towards you and lodging it on your shoulder. I was coughing and still trying to breathe again after your punch, but I wasn't feeling it; the skin of your neck was stretched over my head like a cap and all I could think was ***I might love you, but I'll never like you.***
I couldn't fight any more. My mind saw the back seat as a chance to escape from the deadlock of separate seats, the movie outside, proving ourselves to each other. All those bad films with teenagers at drive-ins, making out in the back; it had to be a better alternative to this. ***Let's see if it's true.*** But when I tried to move, you picked up my head like a melon and bit my mouth, hard, sharp, unhappy, desperate. Fighting me.
You pushed me back, dropped onto me, opened me up. You seemed to have rehearsed this. The gear stick prodded your kidneys. I could feel wet skin but I didn't know if it was yours or mine. I could feel the doorlock button in the back of my neck, and it made my back arch up, lifting you towards the roof, forcing out breath and half-formed words. I began to feel lost, an unfamiliar confusion, fearful. You pushed hard against my hips, sliding with me, pushing me into a panic full of knives and mirrors, a brightness, a sweetness, a liquid state, a failure of will. A return to darkness, distraction, thirst.
For a moment it seemed like the only thing to do next was to button ourselves up and watch the film.
And after some hesitation, when silently we mutually decid-

ed not to speak, that's what we did. You tried to smile, tried to look strong and attentive. We both knew it didn't work. I wanted to try, to make the attempt at feeling close to you for both our sakes. I held your cheekbone in my palm like a pebble, ran a finger through your cold eyelashes, smoothed down your eyebrow hairs, outlined your hairline with my knuckle, pushed my fingers over your scalp, against the direction of your hair, knowing the ache I had provoked near your crown by the wrinkling of your eyelids. I began to feel like it was appropriate to smile. I took a tight grip of some hair and shook your head gently from side to side like a triumphant executioner. And then, what we had been waiting for, hoping for, pushing and fighting for, finally happened. I pulled back my arm. You lashed your neck to the side. Your head and my hand leapt apart. The rip had the sound of a scream, but also of an eye blinking. The precision of our movements made me gasp. Instantaneously, when we snapped ourselves apart at that exact moment, we became equal. All that came before was now irrelevant. An agreement made in action, an action that we both unknowingly made with each other in a second of moving apart, now sealed us.

We had missed too much of the film to bother with the rest. You started up and we drove fast and bumpily down the track and out of the glow of the film in the late dusk. You skidded us back onto the road and accelerated, winding down the window to catch bullets of rain as they shot in through the cold square of space. You were smiling as though you'd just been handed a gift. You were driving hard, angry and joyful, with adrenalin and relief. I absorbed our speed like cold vodka. The gift of your hair, the souvenir of your blood, I held these tight like a lucky charm. ***Go faster***, I said, ***go faster. FASTER.***

>>>

Rush

by Simon Lewis

ONE: CYBERDELIC

'Like a Virgin' crackles from the stereo and I come onto the stage dressed in a nun's habit with a big metal crucifix hanging round my neck. I've unfocused my eyes and the pub is a blur of dark colours and lurid bright spots. The bar is a cage of light at the other side of the room. The shape inside it is Trudy, the only other woman out there. The faces of the audience are pink blobs. I find it easier, to start with, if I can't see the punters. Everything's misty and vague like I'm deep underwater.

"Put your hands together gentlemen," the manager warbles throatily into a mike, "for salacious sister Cecilia, here to save your souls." Some clapping. Someone wolf whistles.

Last night, after it was over, we didn't get to sleep for ages. Fain kept looking in the mirror at his swollen, newly broken nose. I told him it suited him.

Dawn broke; light filtered under the blanket we use as a curtain, illuminating the high walls with picture rails, the expensive, peeling wallpaper, the cardboard boxes where we keep our stuff. Birds started twittering. Fain looked out of the window into the tangled mess of the garden.

"When I was a kid," he said, "you used to see all these colourful birds around. Now all you get are these wrecky pigeons and sparrows." He stubbed a fag into an ashtray already choked with butts. "Crusty birds. Drongos. They look like fucking tramps."

"Survival of the fittest," I said. "The pretty ones didn't have what it takes."

"What are we going to do now?" He asked. "What are we going to do?"

Under the music I can hear a muttering TV, glasses put down on tables, the thok thok of pool balls. Human shapes move from the bar to the chairs and tables.

To start with I'm just standing there for a while. My arms are outstretched and my head is thrown back. I'm supposed to look like I'm having a vision. It was my boss, Screaming Reggie's suggestion. "Put a bit of soul into it," he said. "Believe it. You're a performer, remember. You're an artist."

I have this this ability to let my body run on automatic while my mind goes off and does its thing. It's something I learnt in school, maybe that's why I never did very well there. It's quite a talent, and it's proved more useful than O-levels. My friends can tell when I drift off; my eyes glaze like a window steaming up. When I do it here, they don't mind. I think they like it. They don't want you to be real, human. Vacant is good. Empty is what they come here to see.

I talk to my psychiatrist. She sits in an office in a skyscraper inside my head, and she looks like me but squarer. I tell her my story. She makes notes on a pad. "And then?" she says, "And then?"

Yesterday, Friday, didn't start out like it was going to be much different than usual.

I struggled out of bed about two pm and blew my nose. Every day it's the same. I wake up with a head full of glue. Doctors give me pills and inhalers but nothing makes a difference. They reckon I've got an allergy. Yeah, to getting up maybe. I used about thirty tissues trying to clean out the chemical effluent in my sinuses.

Breakfast was a Silk Cut Light and the pill. I sat down in front of the cracked mirror propped against the wall, pulled my makeup kit out of a cardboard box and started swearing.

Fain grunted awake, gormless, open mouthed. "Spunkstain." I slapped on moisturiser. A new spot was growing on my chin. Foundation. "Shitshovel." Major reconstruction required round the eyes. Eyeliner. I turned in profile and squinted. Jesus Christ, my nose. "Fuckaduck." My nose is a joke. Craggy and hooked, it should belong to a cartoon witch. It messes up my whole face. It's not fair. By rights I should have been a beautiful person. I've got the mind of a beautiful person. But my nose... it's not mine. There's been a mistake. Sometimes I think my whole life has been stymied by my lack of decent nose.

"I like watching you makeup," said Fain, "like an actor getting into character."

"Are you going to get up?" I asked.

"I got up yesterday."

Neither of us are very talented at daytimes.

"Cuntbubbles."

I got the costume from a theatre shop. It was a bad choice – the habit's itchy and it's a bitch to lug about the place. But it was cheap, and the guy threw the cross in for free. Screaming Reggie chose my name.

"Your English enthusiast wants a moniker," he explained, "that he can really wrap his tongue around. One that evokes a continental sexiness, with a sensuous, slippery quality." I asked him what was wrong with Sal. He said it was a petty diminutive, the name of the girl next door who works in a chip shop. Once I met a girl who'd worked in the States, and over there they all called themselves things like Kate and Emma and Jane. She'd even met one who'd called herself Sal.

Reggie is a fat ugly queer who sweats over a fax and a telephone in Soho, sending his 'little angels', as he calls us, all over London. I cover the East End mostly.

I'm in the 'Stag and Hunter' now, or 'Hag and Punter' as we call it. It's a dive.

I drop to my knees, put my hands together and make like I'm praying.

Fain lay in bed with the covers pushed down to his crotch. He looked pretty. He's got a sweet fleshy face, framed with dreads. He looks the way you think babies are going to look when they grow up. He's got this ridiculous cutesy nose, the one I should have got, which is pretty funny, cos he wants mine. He wants to look mean and wasted, not cute.

Fain wants to be taken seriously. He's an Increased Leisure Citizen, but if you met him at a party he'd try to give the impression that he does a lot of dodgy things he can't tell you about. He fancies himself as a bit of a gangsta. Actually, he might tell you he was a DJ. Or a ufologist, depending on how late it was.

With one hand he caressed his Baby Jesus. Fain's Baby Jesus is one of the things I like about him. He's a pretty skinny guy but he's got this big, pregnant belly. He saw me watching him.

"I can feel it kicking!" he said, and patted it.

"Like a vir-ir-ir gin, touched for the very first time–"

There's something wrong with the balance on the stereo. It sounds like karaoke. Once, I asked the manager to put some decent music on for me to perform to, a bit of techno or happy house to liven me up. "No way," he said. "I'm not having that druggy music in my establishment."

I take the crucifix in my hand. I close my eyes and put its tip in my mouth. It tastes sharp and bitter. I run my tongue down its length.

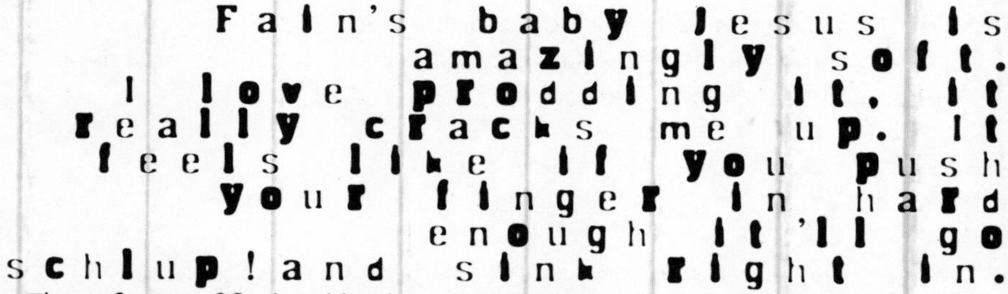

Fain's baby Jesus is amazingly soft. I love prodding it. It really cracks me up. It feels like if you push your finger in hard enough it'll go schlup! and sink right in.

The softness of flesh is like this secret that everybody keeps. You'd never think the people here were made of it. They look and act like they're made out of some harder, more durable stuff, something less vulnerable to time and pain, less easily scarred.

"You have to get up today," I pointed out. "Party tonight."

I met Fain at Planet Nine but we didn't get together till Dreamscape and it wasn't really serious till Karma, when I fell into his lap in tears and asked if I could crash at the squat for a while, till I got my shit together. That was after my dad kicked me out for being irresponsible. Before that I was living with this guy Rigby, but that didn't work out, and before that I was living, I dunno, somewhere else with someone else, it doesn't matter. I've lived a lot of places.

Fain came round to my dad's house with a shopping trolley. We loaded it with my stuff and trundled it across the city. It veered around the pavement, startling pedestrians.

Fain intended to take the trolley back to the interlocking line outside Tescos, and reclaim his one pound coin. But he never got round to it, and it sat for ages in the second floor drawing room, among the skeletal remains of bicycles, until one day we came home wrecked and rolled it down the street. It hit a car and nearly caused an accident and we ran back into the house, giggling.

"I'll get up in a minute," Fain mumbled, "I want to get some lying down done first."

I undo the large button at the top of the habit and shimmy my shoulders about, revealing a strip of pink skin. I'll be glad to get out of this thing; I tripped on the bottom of the material once and fell flat, which is pretty dangerous from this height. In these ridiculous shoes – vicious stilettos – I feel too far from the ground. And my ankles hurt.

I wouldn't say that I enjoyed my job. Aspects of it really piss me off, like having to spend about an hour putting all this makeup on. I even have to smear foundation on my arse, to cover up a few blemishes down there. And there's having to get out of bed and cope with the tube. And there's all the shit attitudes I have to cope with. It's quite a negative thing to do really, and all in all I'd rather be watching TV. But then I guess I wouldn't go a bomb on working behind a checkout either.

I lined my false nails up on the floor.

"Ring Kay," I said.

"Not now."

"Yes now."

Blokes think girls can't throw. Well I can; I chucked the mobile from across the room, which is quite a way, and it landed splat on Fain's stomach. He grumbled and whinged.

"It's very important," I reminded him. "Plee-eese."

He sighed and punched digits. I started sticking the plastic lozenges over my bitten fingernails.

"Alright Kay, it's Fain." A pause. "No, Fain. Fain. Remember?"

"Has Edward come round to see you lately...no, Edward, not Harry. I don't want to know about Harry. Edward. Mr Edward."

I cut the ends of the plastic into oval points. He nodded and grunted into the phone.

"Me and my girlfriend will come round to see you later, yeah? About four. We'll bring the papers. You can show me your collection...yeah. Bye."

"Well?" I said. "Is he holding?"

"He said that Edward came round for a game of Doom and left a pack of Smarties."

"What does that mean?"

"Fuck knows. He's getting so paranoid, he changes the codes every month."

"Is it yes or no?"

"Yes. I think yes." I waved my fingers at his face, like I was casting a spell, waiting for the glue to dry.

"So it's all set up," I said.

Before I did this I had a job in an office. What a nightmare that was. I don't even want to think about it. I had to sit in front of a VDU all day, staring into blue infinity, typing addresses. I got repetitive strain injury after like, two hours. And they expected me to do it virtually all the time five days out of every seven! And they paid me pocket money. 'Well fuck this,' I thought. Thanks, but I'd rather have a life.

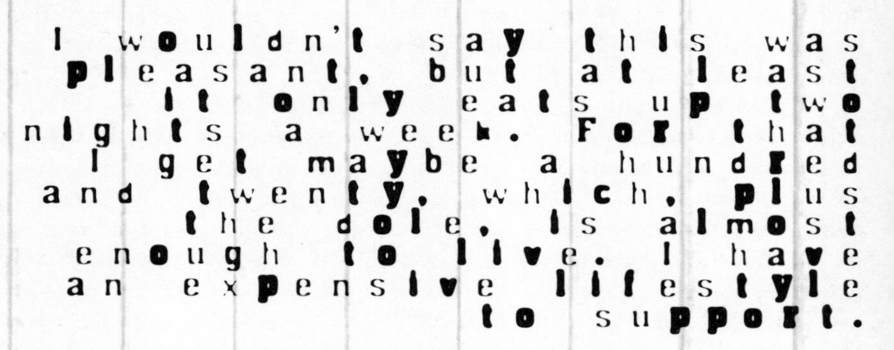

I wouldn't say this was
pleasant, but at least
it only eats up two
nights a week. For that
I get maybe a hundred
and twenty, which, plus
the dole, is almost
enough to live. I have
an expensive lifestyle
to support.

I started looking through the boxes on my side of the bed. Makeup, tapes, a few books, clothes, cuddly toys. Fain's boxes, on his side, contain mostly comics, records, and children's games. Fain's mixing decks sit by the door. We don't have any furniture. It's one of those things I keep meaning to get round to.

Actually we have lots of furniture, but I refuse to use a dead woman's things. The house is huge and draughty with three floors. It used to belong to this mad old girl who copped it. Fain's squatted here for ages; no one knows who owns the place. When I first moved in Fain was still using all her stuff. On my first night here I slept in her bed with her hot water bottle still sat under it.

At two in the morning I asked Fain how she had died. "Peacefully," he said. "At home."

"In this bed!" I screamed. Gross. I leapt out and stood naked on the thick carpet. Pictures of old men with moustaches frowned down at me.

I spent the rest of the night on the couch. The next day I went out and got a new mattress. We put all the dead old woman's stuff in the dining rooms downstairs and shut the doors and forgot about it.

Being well dressed and having a good time is not cheap. My overheads are huge. Look at the cost of the average weekend.

Travelcards. Entrance fees. The price of a decent E these days is a scandal. Fags. Maybe another E. Minicabs. Then dope. A film. An Indian. Phonecalls. More dope. Fifty quid, and that's if I don't go shopping. But it's the little things that all add up: bread, banana milk, crisps, Nutrament, chewing gum, strawberry milk, chips, tights... I hate having to buy tights all the time. One little accident on the dance-floor, one bummer burn, and that's it, another fiver down.

I found the Kwik Save bag I was looking for. It was full of money. Six hundred quid. The result of months of hard graft and discipline. Saving up was an unpleasant experience, all that self denial and discipline, and one I would not want to repeat. But it was in a good cause.

I stood on the bed, straddling Fain's naked chest, and emptied it over him. The rumpled notes tumbled out and drifted over his naked chest, onto the bed, onto the floor, and lay there like litter. I pointed a long-nailed finger at his face. "We," I said, "have to go and invest this."

He smiled.

"Artificial girl," he said. "My, what big claws you've got," and pulled me down.

I undo another button on the habit and it drops to the floor. I step out of its black puddle, exposing my second uniform, the usual packaging, a lot of complicated underwear. My body is sectioned and split with lines of silk and nylon.

Fain is one of the few people I've met with the same dedication to having a good time that I've got. Most people, I figure, don't enjoy enjoying themselves. Miserable is less effort.

Fain and I, we aren't truly madly deeply, but we get on alright. We go well together. It's low maintenance and few running costs. Course I wouldn't say no to undying love and to have and to hold and faith and loyalty, but I'm dealing with men here, not dogs.

Increasingly I hear our friends refer to us together, as if our names have fused: Fainansal. It sounds harsh and German. Salanfain. I like that better. I think that's a brand of French margarine. Salanfain.

TWO: UFORIA

The record stops and there is a moment of silence. Just for a second I stand and catch my breath. I become very conscious of what I am, a half naked human being standing on a stage. I look down. Then the speakers crackle and 'Material girl' starts playing and I'm off again, swaying and jigging, but faster now.

We met the blind man in the corridor outside Kay's flat, on the top floor of a Brixton council block. He was standing with his hands on the waist high balcony, his face pointing out over the view. He stiffened as we approached. At first I thought he had vertigo; only when he turned towards us and seemed to be staring at my ear did I realise he was blind. I stopped.

"You a friend of Kay?" said Fain.

"I know him."

He turned his head. He was young, and dressed like the estate kids, baggy jeans, trainers, earrings. "Tell me," he said, "What do you see?" We looked out over the view. Below was the concrete maze of the estate. Children played on bright climbing frames in ordered squares of grass. Beyond that was a spikey, geometric plain.

"You can see Big Ben and the houses of Parliament and the Post Office Tower," said Fain.

"Just buildings, buildings," I said. "It looks like a jumble of angles."

"What do you see?" I asked him.

"I see blurred shapes and colours," he said. "No detail. All I can see is the sky. From here the sky is huge." I looked again. The sky was pale blue with accents of pink and purple. The colours were unconvincing, bad taste.

"Is Kay in?" said Fain.

"Yeah."

I fingered the wad of notes in my pocket. I carried the money; Fain said I was less likely to be mugged. Fain rattled Kay's letter box and the door opened. We left the blind man with his sky.

"And what I'm saying–" I can hear two blokes at the front. The shorter, balder one is leaning over the table lecturing his fatter, hairier companion. "What I'm saying is, if they spend all their time locked up, staring at pictures of this bloke in a g-string hanging off a cross, they're going to get ideas is what I'm saying."

"God's tarts."

"Yeah," the fatter, hairier one is nodding, "minge of the messiah."

Kay was a small guy with a lot of hair. We sprawled on cushions at his feet. He sat in an armchair in the centre of the room, like an Egyptian statue, lord of all he surveyed, which was four unpainted walls, some car stereos, a scattering of comics and discarded packaging on the floor, a Roland 303, dirty windows, an Omega, a bare mattress, and a CD Rom games system.

He spoke like a head of state making pronouncements. "I went shopping today and the bill came to twenty three pounds twenty three," he said. "I wrote my car off once on the A23. I have 23 volumes of 2000ADs. The number 23 bus comes down my road."

"I'm twenty three," said Fain.

"How old are you Sal?" asked Kay.

"Twenty."

"Oh. I believe in coincidences," said Kay, waving a joint around for emphasis. Smoke drifted languidly in the stale air, forming a plateau above our heads.

I kick my shoes off. Lying flat on the stage they look like weapons. I turn my head to the side and I can see a white blur sitting on the chair in the wings, smoking a fag. That's Annaliese. She is on after me. I take comfort from her presence – with all this male energy, this testosterone, hanging in the air, it's good to feel there is another woman around.

I met her earlier in the dressing room – the ladies loo. She was doing coke when I came in. The first thing I thought when I saw her was, that girl's got a hooter like a vacuum cleaner.

Just on first impressions I could tell she'd got a bit of a problem.

Fain and Kay played Robowarriors. Already bored, I flicked through books and comics.

"What have you been doing the last few months?" Kay asked.

"I've been to a lot of Restart interviews," said Fain. "I don't know how they expect you to find time to get a job, all the stuff they make you do. Jobclubs, back to work plans. And it's not as if I sign on under that many names."

Kay nodded sympathetically.

"I signed on as a painter and decorator," continued Fain. "Now they're hassling me, saying, how can you have not found any work for two years as a painter and decorator? They were going to cut my dole. I only got out of it by saying no one would hire me cos I was so incompetent."

"I told them I was a shepherd," said Kay. "I figure there's not a great demand for shepherds in Stockwell."

"Outlaw bandits of the future," said the computer in a metallic drawl, over and over.

"I'm an actress really."

Annaliese, in a nurses uniform, hunched over the tiles with a tenner up her nose. I watched her hoover a line. She's got burst blood vessels around the base of her nostrils. It's a shame to see a good nose go to waste like that. I started getting changed, hoping she was feeling generous.

"What's the crowd like?" she asked.

"Pretty lively."

"Good. I hate it when they're all half asleep, watching the football."

She straightened and sniffed.

"I perform better stoned," she said, waving the tenner. "It gives me an edge. I'm pretty good actually. I get a lot of applause."

I thought of a joke about standing ovations but kept it to myself.

"Want some?" she said.

'At last,' I thought.

"What was that blind guy after?" I asked.

Kay didn't take his eyes from the busy screen. "He wanted to hire a gun."

"How much is a gun?"

"Fifty a week," said Fain. He was always keen to show off his knowledge of such things. "Plus two hundred deposit. When you return it you get an extra twenty discount if it still contains all the ammo."

"But I don't do that shit," said Kay. "I told him to try the 3rd floor."

"3rd floor, guns," said Fain, "4th floor, videos. 5th floor, ladies underwear."

"But he was blind," I said.

Kay shrugged. "That's his problem." He waved a crisp packet at me. "Want a Mr Munchie?"

I slide off a stocking. I'm looking out into the cluster of eggs and I'm wondering if any of them have seen me before. I think of a story Annaliese told me.

"I used to have this bloke, a fan, followed me around from gig to gig." She started chopping a line. "Always there at the front, mouth slightly open, real attentive. Appreciative. He used to clap." Chop chop chop. "One day I come out, ta da, go into the naughty nurse routine, and he's sitting there and there's a woman sitting next to him. I don't think anything of it. Then after the show, he manages to get backstage. He knew the manager or something. He pokes his head round the door. 'Annaliese,' he says – I don't know how he knew my name, but I didn't like it– 'Annaliese, I want you to meet my wife.' And he pushes open the door and they're both standing there, holding hands, grinning."

"What did they want?" I asked.

"I don't know. I slammed the door in their faces and called the bouncer."

Chop chop. "Never saw him again."

The men sat wiggling their joysticks, stopping occasionally to roll joints and eat.

Kay glanced at one of the books I had been reading. I was too monged to read now; I looked at the pictures in the comics.

"Jesus was a spaceman," he said, his lips flecked with grains of Cheesy Bites. "It's well known in certain circles but the knowledge is suppressed by the CIA. The ascension into heaven? More like return to the mothership. Miracles? I don't think so. Modern medicine, anti-grav belts, matter transformers."

"Totally," said Fain.

KABBOW! There was a picture of a big explosion and men running. Decka decka decka went the guns. "Stack!" said a Nort. "He wears no mask!"

"I knew this girl," I told Annaliese, waving the tenner around. "She was going out with this guy. He was sweet, but straight. Worked in an office. They were in love. She was afraid to tell him what she did. So she said she worked in a box office.

That explained the weird hours. She left the flat wearing a suit. At work she got changed, put her makeup on. It worked for months. He never suspected a thing. Then one day she's working a pub in the Old Kent Road. Real dive. She's on stage with a dildo. And he walks in with his work mates, sits down. They catch each other's eye. There's nothing she can do. She has to keep going to the end." I snorted awhile.

"And?" said Annaliese.

I shrugged. "And nothing. Far as I know they're still together."

"How much do you want?" asked Kay. 'At last,' I thought.

"A hundred and twenty," said Fain. Kay reached under a chair and pulled out a bag of capsules. Dutch ecstasy, apparently.

"That's a lot more than usual," he said.

Fain shrugged. "I'm expanding."

"We want to start our own club," I said. "We need a lot of capital. We think about two grand should be enough to start us off."

"What are you going to call it?" asked Kay, counting pills out onto the table.

"X-cubed," said Fain.

"Fish," I said, "or Seaweed."

"Ten, twelve, fourteen, sixteen..."

"It's going to be totally new and original," I said.

"Louder," said Fain.

"Faster," I said.

"Twenty two, twenty four, twenty six.."

"Much harder."

"Thirty two..thirty four, thirty six.."

"We want it to be really out there," said Fain, "extreme."

I take off my other stocking. It is thin and insubstantial in my hand. I let it drop. What is this thing with underwear? It's all the same. I asked Annaliese about it. "Men aren't very complicated," she said. "I mean they're more complicated than say–" she looked round for inspiration, "a Tampax machine. But not as complicated as a CD player."

"A Tibetan monk can commit suicide by repeating two phrases," said Kay as he shovelled the pills into another plastic bag. I took the money out. "The first, 'hic', opens a hole in the top of their head." He sealed the bag and passed it over to Fain. I gave Fain the wad and he gave it to Kay. "The second, 'phat', releases the soul, which flies out the hole and bums about in the air. An amazing people..."

Oh, oh, I thought, here we go. Kay was notorious for forcing people to listen to his boring travel stories. How at 16, fresh-faced and naive, he had hitched out of New Cross with nothing but a guitar and sunglasses and a hundred trips sewn into the lining of his jacket. How he had lived in Danish anarchist collectives, experimenting with lifestyles in harmony with the earth, and selling the trips at twenty quid a time. How he had then felt the call of the mysterious East, and had travelled into the depths of the Himalayas, to seek out Tibetan refugees in their mountain villages and buy kilos of charice off them; how he had sold that on the palm-fringed beaches of Goa, where he lived for six months, having affairs with dusky, exotic maidens, mostly Israeli package tourists. And so on.

Kay's voice tailed off. He fingered the mone, seeming to forget we were there for a moment. "You know, I sure could do with some of that Tibetan stuff." He waved his arm at the window, the view. "I can't be doing with this shit any more."

I start to undo the lace on the back of my basque.

Annaliese had done it up for me in the dressing room a little earlier.

"Here we go again," I said, when she had finished.

"At least it keeps you fit."

"How long are you going to do this for?" I asked.

"Till something better comes along. I have got a career. I've had walk-ons in The Bill and London's Burning." She looked hard at herself.

"How long have you been doing it?"

"About four years," she said, adjusting her little hat. "Maybe five."

"We have to go now," I said, and stood up shakily. I'd heard enough for one day. Fain saw Kay as a good role model, feeling that his simple existence – sell drugs, eat, watch TV, take drugs, sleep, read – was admirably monkish. But me, I just thought he was weird, and I figured you couldn't do what he did without being a bit of a cunt on the sly.

"Be seeing you man." Kay gave Fain a hug. "And you man." He said to me. He shook my hand.

I blinked as I stepped outside into the sobering blasts of air. It was getting dark. The sky was purple and blue like a bruise. I patted the plastic bag of pills secreted down my bra.

The basque drops to the floor.

'Five years,' I thought. I couldn't imagine it.

"I wouldn't mind," said Annaliese, "if it wasn't for the smell. You get this pubby smell and it sticks to all your clothes and it gets in your house and your bed and you just can't get rid of it." I opened the door to leave. "You can't get rid of it."

Back home we got ready to go out. I painted my nails green. Fain said they looked poisonous. We stood together in front of the mirror in the hallway. My hair was done up in pigtails, his dreads fanned out from a high ponytail so his head looked like a pineapple. We both wore black bomber jackets. My red crop top (no logo) showed a thin slither of skin before the rim of my leather skirt. The end of his floppy t-shirt flapped about the thigh pockets of his combat trousers. The tongues of my Caterpillar Boots pointed rudely outwards. His knackered Five Stars hugged the ground discreetly. We looked at each other looking at ourselves. I imagined us as a couple you'd see in one of the more underground fashion mags. A lurid polaroid, our faces white, with trendy red eye. We went well together.

Fain tucked a bag holding fifty of the pills down his Calvin Kleins."Ready," he said.

I wiggle my hips about and slide my knickers down. I've got a g-string on underneath. One night, Fain tried to get me to wear my work clothes to bed. I explained quietly: "I don't mix business and pleasure." Being in bed together, it should be like a hot tub of skin and feelings. I don't want it to be like another bloody porn emporium. I don't want to watch Fain watching. I don't want to see him like I see the punters, with that expression on his face.

I found an E in my jacket in the taxi. In a matchbox. Been there for weeks. But I'm terrible with drugs – one day I'll to get round to vacuuming the carpet and I won't need to buy draw for weeks, I'll just skin up the contents of the hoover bag.

I split the pill with a long green nail and we necked it right there in the cab.

I could already feel my stomach lurching in preparation. Party party. I ground my teeth and watched the car headlights eat up the road.

Come on, come on. It was raining and people dashed along the pavement looking pissed off. I entertained myself by checking out the fashion crimes. What was it like to wear green trainers and a yellow cardigan and not to care? Come on, come on. Party party party.

"You wear that shit," I told Fain that night, pointing at the bundle of black underwear. So he did. He looked so funny with it on. The panties bulging like a holster, the hairs on his legs sticking out through the holes in the fishnets. Actually he looked kind of sexy. "Funny man," I said, "come here."

THREE: IMPULSATIONS

The music changes abruptly. The last line of *Material Girl* is choked off by the start of *Justify My Love*. The sudden switch is awkward, jarring.

I shimmy about for a while and jiggle my tits.

I let my eyes refocus and appraise the hunched punters. They sit calm with their pints. Some of them look like they've been hypnotised. Others are just carrying on with the usual pub stuff, stealing the occasional glance. It's a good crowd. They'll be worth at least fifty, maybe even a hundred.

A guy shrunk in a dark corner has started jerking off under the table. They think you can't tell; but the expression on their faces gives them away, and the tension around their neck,, and their enormous hungry eyes.

"Free as the air that I bree-eathe!"

The refrain, a fragment from a torch song spliced into the thumping techno, went round and round inside my head like a marble in a cup.

I danced under a fluorescent fish, pigtails bobbing. It was dark and smoky. Beams of light swept over the crowd, momentarily illuminating an outstretched hand, a rapt and sweaty face. Ultraviolet paintings glowed in unearthly colours around the walls of the hall. A green laser drew geometric shapes in the air. On the stage a DJ crouched in a cockpit of synthesisers, decks and monitors. Screens above his head showed fractal landscapes, explosions, computer generated cows, riot police, tribal dances, F1-11s.

The music was so loud I felt like I was hearing it with my whole body; the beat was the thumping of my heart, the flow of blood around my veins, the rhythm of my thoughts. I closed my eyes and let it jerk me. I liked the anonymity of the crowd, being crammed into a dense mass of bodies. I was communing with something larger than me. I was one element in an amorphous mass of whirling limbs and pumping torsos, one particle in a ceaseless explosion. I was transported, elevated. And nicely wasted.

"Free as the air that I bree-eathe!"

At the Stag and Hunter the ceiling is stained gold with tobacco. Eye of the Tiger, flashes the pinball machine. I can read the signs behind the bar:

Do not ask for credit as a punch in the mouth often offends.
Users of mobile phones will be asked to leave. No spitting.

A thick heavy silence has settled on the room. There is a cluster of young men around the pool table. One guy slowly chalks his cue.

I was standing at the bar, waiting to be ripped off for a bottle of water, when I felt this hand on my neck. It was Rigby, my ex-lover, grinning like a maniac and shuffling about in his sandals. We exchanged cautious hellos. The last time I saw him I was chucking kitchen utensils at his head.

"You still stripping?" he asked.

"Yeah," I said. Rigby knew I didn't like talking about it in public. "You still taking advantage of gullible middle aged women?"

Rigby was into all that New Age bollocks.

He worked on 0898 Tarot line. He sat in an office and read people's cards for them over the phone at 44p a minute. I used to think it was a cool job until I realised he actually believed the shit he was dishing. He told me their auras went down the optic cables.

I had to admit he was looking good. Rigby was everything you could want in a bloke until he opened his mouth.

We gave each other dirty looks. This conversation, it was like when two dogs meet in the park and circle round each other growling and being butch and sniffing each others arses.

He chose to ignore my remark.

"You know where I can get any pills?"

"Ask my boyfriend. He's hanging out in the lobby."

"You go out with a dealer? That must be convenient for you." "How's your love life?" I asked. "Has Marie Antoinette come across yet? Or Cleopatra?"

When I met him he told me we were lovers in a previous life. I've heard worse first lines. I moved in with him after two weeks. It lasted for a couple of months, until the day I came home and found him shagging the spirit of a Mesopatamian High Priestess on the kitchen work surface. This priestess must have built up some shit karma when she was around, for her to be reincarnated in the body of my ex-best friend Julie. Julie was so dizzy I'm amazed she didn't fall over all the time. Most of the time she was rowing with only one oar. I mean, several cans short of a sixpack. And she had fat ankles. Actually, as I thought about it then, I realised I did kind of miss her.

"What's he like, your latest guy?"

"He's kind and considerate and..."

"I mean what does he look like? I want to score."

I dance about the stage in my g-string. Sometimes I pull down one of the straps then let it slip back into place.

Reggie insisted I draw this out for as long as possible.

"Stripping is not about getting naked," he said. "It's about frustration. It's about deferral of gratification. Nudity is boring, and not very sexy."

W H E E E E Y Y Y Y Y Y Y Y Y Y O O O O O O O O O O O O O O O O O !

I rushed down an infinite tunnel at speed. Blue sparks flew. I was driving a Ferrari into the centre of the universe. The tunnel walls pulsed. My mind was empty, It didn't exist, there was just the punch of the bass and the bang bang bang of the beat.

"Stop it," said Fain. He pulled my fingers away from my eyelids. I blinked the room back into place. We sat grinding our jaws in a pool of ultraviolet light in the corner of the hall. The whites of Fain's eyes glowed eerily. A sheen of sweat stood out on his face. He couldn't stop smiling, revealing his luminous teeth.

"I was getting well into that," I yelled.

"I want us to be together," he roared into my ear.

We looked into each others faces. I began to stroke the soft, downy material of Fain's top. I made my smile bigger. He looked so beautiful, and the top was like the soft fur of a big fluffy cat.

We hugged each other. Fain brushed his hands over the nylon on my legs. The sensation of his fingers was like, wow, electricity. With his other hand he gripped my waist. I felt warm and secure and completely off my face. He let his hand dawdle down towards the bright joy of my shoelaces. We purred at each other.

I put my hand inside his top. He caught his breath as I tweaked a nipple.

"Did you sell all the pills?" I shouted.

"Yeah, easy." He tapped his crotch, where he stashed the profits. He squeezed the wad of cash through his trousers. "Seven hundred quid," he said.

"Cool," I shouted. "Let me feel."

Someone should lecture the guy in the corner about deferral of gratification.

I look out into the tobacco colours of the pub and all I see is the double dots of eyes, like I'm looking in a forest and it's night and the animals are gathering.

Maybe it was three in the morning. That time of night when nothing matters much any more. The rest of your life is a million miles away, and daylight won't happen for a few years yet.

I sat copping off with Fain in the corner of the chill out room. The music was soft and low and moved in wistful spirals, like the smoke from the joss sticks in the wall. Ambient's not my packet of crisps, and this stuff sounded like a humpback whale playing the didgereedoo, but it's a lot easier to snog to than techno, you don't feel the urge to tap your feet and wag your tongue in time. The first E was wearing off, but things were still pretty rosy, like even sitting in a puddle of spilled beer wasn't an unpleasant sensation. I'd just taken one of Fain's and was expecting to come up soon.

Fain was making contented noises. Over his shoulder I could see flaked out ravers sprawled over beanbags like accident victims. A pair of teeny crusties sat on the speakers, banging on bongos. "Sorry we're not computers," sang one of them. A couple chatted by the designer bar, where you could buy juice spiked with something American that made you smarter. If you were willing to pay three quid for an orange juice you probably needed it. She had red hair and wore a silver dress. In the undersea light her skin looked blue.

'Loveheart' said her t-shirt. 'The aliens are coming to save the earth' said his. She was nodding vigorously as he talked about transcendental meditation. She looked fascinated, like it was her favourite subject at school. Who was she trying to fool? Sometimes conversation is just the dullest kind of foreplay.

There's some really wrecky looking blokes in here. Old guys with wrinkled skin hanging baggy on their bones like badly fitting clothes. But their eyes are bright. They hardly seem to blink. Wherever I move I carry their eyes with me. It's heavy, the pressure of all those gazes. It feels like heat.

Oh no. Rigby again. He tapped Fain on the shoulder and crouched down. We separated, a string of saliva briefly running between our lips.

"What do you want?" I asked.

Fain sat up, giving himself more height.

"Hello there," said Rigby. "Having a good time?"

"Yeah, we were,". said Fain.

"Sal's a good kisser, isn't she? I'd give her an eight."

The two men glared at each other. Suddenly there was all these macho hormones buzzing in the air.

"I wanted to do you a favour," said Rigby. He looked at me.

"For old time's sake."

"You–," he pointed at Fain, "are not popular. There's a lot of people downstairs getting very pissed off." He leaned closer. "Those pills of yours don't work."

"Oh yeah," said Fain. "Maybe you're just not doing it right."

"Seriously," he said. "Give me my money back."

"I reckon it's your tough luck."

"No mate, it's yours." I was like, what a stimulating debate. Neanderthal politics.

"Or maybe one of them will ask me where you are and I'll have to tell him. I really wouldn't like to be you when they find you."

I could tell Fain was shaken, but he didn't want to show it.

"Didn't you try them before you started selling?" Rigby asked.

"There wasn't time," said Fain.

"Just give him the money," I said. If I intervened Fain wouldn't lose face. I could see the two of them squaring off all night, going ug ug and banging their clubs on the ground.

"You'll thank me for this," said Rigby.

Fain breathed in and stuck his hand down his trousers, groping round his sweaty bollocks for the bag full of cash.

The guy in the corner is going for it now, all caution chucked away. He looks like he's desperate for the loo but can't go. His face! It makes me laugh.

We decided to leave quickly. But you had to go through all the other rooms to get out. People recognised Fain and came up to demand their cash. He handed out tenners. Sorry, sorry. Angry faces floated out of the crowd to confront us. Sorry, sorry, have some money. The atmosphere around us was charged and nasty. Irate ravers, vexed at their unexpected sobriety, shook their fists and waved their heads.

We shoved our way into the main hall. Suddenly we were staring into a redhead, with a shaved, angry looking scalp. I looked into his mouth at the tobacco stains on his teeth. 'Loved Up' said his t-shirt. He punched Fain's face. Fain reeled.

"Oh god, let's get out of here," I wailed. "Just get out." We shoved through the thick mass of limbs. The laser made a level plain of green light over the crowd. Someone put up their hand to break it. Smoke swirled and whirled on its surface and it looked like the surface of a deep lake and the rising hand was the last gesture of a dying man. The smoke stung my eyes. I felt like I could hardly breathe.

Two security men in black with torches swinging on their belts grabbed Fain's elbows.

"You're not welcome here," they said and pulled him along, into the lobby. I followed, and watched them throw him out the door into the dark.

The cross hangs down between my tits. It jumps up and down as I dance, and sometimes it hurts. It has given me bruises in the past.

My elbows and knees are aching from where I've hit the floor. It's hard work this, it's heavy manual labour.

It was cold outside. Fain leant against the railings. His face was pale, with a Hitler moustache of blood. He clutched his nose. It had recently stopped raining and the tarmac glistened, reflecting the acid glow of streetlights and neon. The middle distance was a jumble of spots and daubs of artificial light. Fain once said the streets at night were his favourite landscape, in tune with his usual state of mind.

"I'm going to Kay's," he said. "He ripped me off."

People were still queuing to get inside. They watched us silently. "I think my nose is broken. I could feel it go." His shoulders shook. He waved at a taxi sailing past. It stopped and we climbed inside. I looked back at the queue, a fashionable chain gang. I could still hear the music, but now it was tinny and small. Suddenly I felt very straight.

I slide the g-string down and let it drift onto the stage.

The bloke in the corner twitches and strains. His face bulges. I see him go tense then floppy. Then he looks like he just wants to disappear completely into the darkness. He slugs on his pint and scratches his head. Quietly he places his hands on the table, and looks at them for a while.

FOUR: OXYGENERATE

Even when I'm wearing nothing my body is not empty; it's been customised. There is a tattoo of an orchid, my favourite flower, on my left thigh, and a Chinese character on my ankle. I got that in Greece when I was spun out on some dodgy pills and I still don't know what it means. One of my nipples is scarred, swollen from the time I got it pierced by the body artist in the Angel. I vividly remember the crinkling sound as she pulled on her plastic gloves. "Now I thread the needle through the epidermis," she said. I had to take the ring out after a month as my body rejected it, which pissed me off; who's in charge here, me or my flesh?

And there are the accidental marks, the scars, the burns, the moles, the wrinkles and stretch lines. Here, they want to see skin flawless and smooth like a mannequin's. But bodies are marked, covered in doodles. Bodies are written on. Bodies are stories.

Kay's block, a column of lights, rose into the darkness. The lift carried us to the top floor. Someone had pissed in it recently and it stank. We didn't talk. I read the graffiti. Call Big Ron for a good time. IRA. And a little ditty in the corner in neat capitals: 'I and the public know, what all schoolchildren learn, those to whom evil is done, do evil in return.'

The city was spread out beneath us, a rug of black shapes and lights. The sky was purple, enflamed, smeared with pus-like streaks. Jesus, the fucking sky. When did we screw that up? Kay's door was open. We pushed it and went inside.

I slide the metal chain over my neck. I hold the cross out. I begin to rub it over my body. I close my eyes. I draw patterns with the crucifix on my chest, my thighs.

"Give me your fucking money."

The blind guy stood in the living room, pointing a gun at Kay, who was flattened against the wall, next to an army kit bag. They both seemed pretty wrapped up; neither of them noticed us, stood gaping in the doorway like tourists.

"What if I haven't got any?" said Kay.

"You're going away," he said. "I know you've got loads. And I know it's in here." A pause.

"Where's the money?" Said the blind guy, louder. "Give me the fucking money." His face was all beaten up with stress; armed robbery was really taking it out of him. Kay didn't look too hot either.

"No," whispered Kay. "No."

"I'm serious," said the blind guy. "I'm really fucking serious." His face was pointed over to one side like the whole thing was a bit embarrassing. I guess he was sighting by ear.

Then Kay turned and saw us. "Come in," he said. "Join the party."

I put the crucifix between my legs. I made Fain sand down the corners off the shaft so it doesn't hurt.

I went to yoga classes once. This mellow old hippy taught me how to breathe. You should breathe really low down, really deep.

Hardly anyone knows how to breathe. Apparently, what we do these days, especially in the cities that's not breathing. That's gasping for air.

"Over there!" the blind guy shouted at us. "By the wall." He waved his gun around, pointed it at us in turns, like he couldn't decide who to shoot first. We came in and lined up next to Kay. Fain stuck his hands up in the air, like the kid at school who's busting for a slash.

I concentrate on my breath. I feel air going down into my abdomen. I feel my chest expand, contract. I imagine my body is hollow and full of smoke. When I breathe I breathe the bad smoke out, I breathe the good stuff in.

"Good night?" said Kay and laughed this mad chuckle.

"It was alright," I said.

"Who was playing?" he asked.

"The Woolly Crew," I said.

"Were they any good?" he asked.

"Shut up!" shouted the blind guy.

"Please don't shoot me," said Fain.

"Shut up. Shut up," said the blind guy, and then there was this weird pause like he'd forgotten his lines and everyone stood around like awkward teenagers. I was like, will someone please say something? So I did.

"What's your name?" I went.

I rub myself with the cross. I'm not really here. I'm empty.

The blind guy didn't reply.

"You got a gun then," I said. And I thought, who is this moron with the dumb small talk? But it was like, now I'd said something I just had to keep going.

"Yeah and I can use it. Don't think I can't use it."

"I don't doubt that."

"I've got two arms and two legs. I'm good with my hands. I've got good hearing. I can tell you're wearing leather by the way it rustles. And I can smell good. You're wearing perfume but you've been sweating a lot."

I blushed.

"What do you see?" I said.

"You're a black shape."

"I'm Sal," I said. "Sal." I took a step forward.

"Just because you don't see good, people think you're stupid," he said. "They think you can't do anything. They think you're mental and useless.I get so angry..."

Breathe in light. Breathe out smoke. Breathe in pink, breathe out grey. Breathe in sweet, breathe out sour. The grey light is leaving me. It curls out of my body, all the smoke, all the pollution.

"You haven't done this before, have you?"

"I have so." I took another step forward. Now I was right in front of him. He was only young.

"You won't get away with this," said Kay. "I know this guy, right, knows this guy he'll put a drill through each of your knees for fifty quid. Fifty quid. That's cheap I reckon. That's a bargain. And for a hundred–"

"Shut your face," said the blind guy, waving his gun.

"What are you going to do, shoot me? Then how-" he started laughing. The words stumbled out between giggles. "Then how are you going to find the money?" He creased up with hilarity.

"I think you're very brave," I said. "We all do."

"I guess it takes a certain amount of balls..." said Fain.

"They said I couldn't do this," said the blind guy. "They said I didn't have what it takes. But I do. I can do it. I can."

"Yes you can," I said. "You can." I reached forwards and gently put my hand over his, onto the gun. "Give me the gun," I said. I felt his grip lessen. "Give me the gun and go." And I took it out of his hand.

Breathe in light, breathe out dark. Breathe in happiness and health. Let it be over now. Let it stop.

"Go," I said. He ran out of the room. I heard the door slam.

"Jesus Christ," said Fain, leaning his head back against the wall. "Jesus." The gun was squat and black and surprisingly heavy.

"That guy is fucking dead," said Kay. "He's fucking dead. He's dead meat." There was a long pause. All I could hear was the panting of breath.

"Don't be too hard on him," I said. "He was just ambitious."

"He was mad," said Kay, "that's what he was."

"He was trying to overcome his natural afflictions." I toyed with the gun. My back was still turned. "Maybe he just wanted to be normal."

I turned around. I planted my feet wide apart, like they do in films, and held the gun in both hands, arms outstretched. Sometimes I get these mad ideas that seem brilliant for a quarter of a second but I never do them. Not normally.

'Oh fuck it,' I thought. I've had such a shitty day.

I pointed the gun at Kay.

"Give me all your fucking money!" I said.

I walk to the back of the stage and pick up my collection plate, then step off the stage and onto the floor. I wiggle and sway. I hold the plate out. It's important to catch the eye of each punter as he reaches for his wallet.

"You what?" said Kay. "Don't piss around."

"Give me all your fucking money."

"Sal," said Fain, "what are you doing?"

I flicked the safety catch off. I pointed the gun at the CD-Rom. The trigger was stiff and I had to pull hard. KABLAM! The gun jumped in my hand and the computer blew up with a flash. Cool.

"Jesus Christ." Kay did his nut, waving his arms around and jigging about.

"He's my friend!" said Fain. "You can't mug my friend."

I can see my reflection in the mirrors on the wall. I look thin and very pink. Delicate.

Noise begins again. The men are stirring in their seats.

"He's a scumbag," I said.

"I think that's a bit unfair," said Kay.

Neither of them could believe this. I couldn't either, really, it was like I was having an exciting dream. I didn't know why I was doing this. I was making it up as I went along.

"Why'd you rip us off?" I said.

"I have to go away," said Kay. "I needed the cash. I thought you wouldn't find out till it was too late." He turned to Fain. "Sorry man."

"That was pretty shitty," said Fain.

This made me even madder. So I shot the stereo. KKFOOM! Yeah. Fucking A.

"Next time it's your feet," I shouted. "I've had a bad day, I'm in a shit mood, so give me all your fucking money."

"Okay, okay," said Kay.

"That was beautiful love. Beautiful." A short guy drops a furled tenner on the plate. I give him a smile, then dodge nimbly out the way of his approaching hand. I wiggle my finger. Naughty. You can look, but you can't touch.

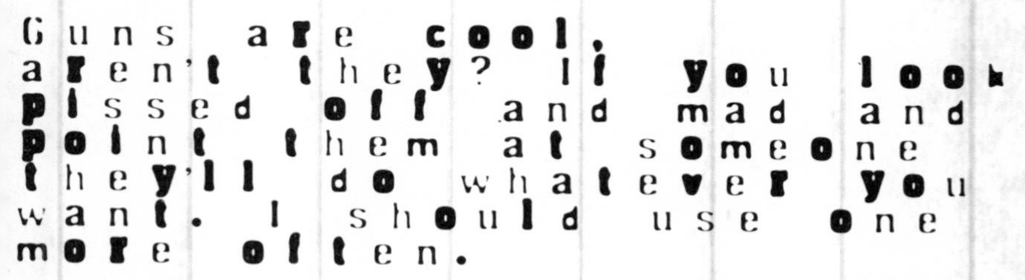

Guns are cool,
aren't they? If you look
pissed off and mad and
point them at someone
they'll do whatever you
want. I should use one
more often.

Kay reached into the kitbag and pulled out a wad of notes. He tossed it to the floor at my feet. There was a plane ticket at the top.

I flicked back the cover of the ticket. Bombay, this morning. Underneath it was a book of travellers cheques, and underneath that a stack of cash.

"You make enemies, doing this," said Kay. "There's some people who want to hurt me. I thought I'd disappear for a while, chill out in India for a year or two. I'm tired of it all Sal," he said. "I'm just really tired."

"So what about all this shit?" I waved the gun at the hardware round the room.

"A mate was coming to buy it."

I threw the plane ticket and travellers cheques back at him, and stuffed the cash in my jacket.

"Have a pleasant trip," I said. "We're going now." Fain jerked like he was dozing and just woke up. He shrugged at Kay and walked over to me. I backed out of the room, still pointing the gun. Then I started running.

The shorter, balder guy shakes his head. "You've got a talent love," he says. He's moved. He looses a fiver. The fatter, hairier one drops a couple of coins.

"Nice one," he says. "Nice one."

"I can't believe you did that." Fain paced up and down and kept repeating himself. "I can't believe it."

"Shut up. I'm trying to count." I sat in the orange light of a bus stop, hunched over the book of notes. It was a real blockbuster, a rip roaring read. I couldn't put it down.

"Four and a half grand," I said, eventually.

"That's a lot," said Fain.

I wished he would say something sensible for a change.

Crisp, autumn coloured tenners, sea blue fivers, squat pound coins glinting gold. My collection plate is filling up. It's a good night. I might even top a hundred. I shimmy over to the wanker in the corner. "Would you like to add your contribution?" I give him the look, full face, and he buckles, won't look me in the eye, and drops me a fiver.

I mounted the stairs of the night bus. I was in shock. Everything looked very solid. The can of Brew rolling back and forth along the aisle was like the most real thing I'd ever seen, full of significance. There was one other guy on the top, curled in a little bundle at the back. His ears looked familiar. I stopped in the aisle and watched him for a while. Maybe the real pisser of being blind is not knowing when others are looking at you. He looked so sad and small,

"Our stop," said Fain. Before I got off I walked over to the guy. He looked up and he smiled warily. Really, he did. I smiled back and then I realised he couldn't see it so I touched his cheek, gently. I peeled a bundle of notes off the wad and dropped it in his lap. I'm a big softie really.

"I think you'll all agree," the manager croons into the mike. "Sister Cecilia excelled there. Sadly she has informed me that that was her last performance. So please show your appreciation for all the good work she's done. A big hand, gentlemen, for Sister Cecilia!"

When I woke up this afternoon I knew something was weird, but for a while I couldn't work out what it was.

I lay dozing. Fain was already up. He was sat by his decks, mixing. I watched him dozily as he mixed the two tracks, sliding different sounds together, cooking music with deft movements of his fingers. He looks cute when he's working, he sticks his tongue out the corner of his mouth.

He saw that I was awake.

"We should talk about what we're going to do now," he said. "Are we gonna get this club together or what?"

"Maybe we should go away for a while first," I said.

I sat up in bed and then I realised what it was. My nose wasn't blocked.

Now, I reckon it must have been Kay's pills, rejects from some bungled pharmacy raid. But at the time it was like this miracle had happened. It felt like this huge weight had dropped from my face. I closed my eyes and breathed deeply through my nostrils and it was like I was breathing for the first time. The rush of air made me dizzy. Wow. Fresh air. Now that is some good shit.

"What do you want to be up so early for?" I told Fain. "Get back to bed."

A ripple of applause begins. I take a bow, flash a smile, and scoop up my clothes. Then I'm gone.

planting seeds

H I L A I R E

She worked in a basement. It was cold, especially in the summer, due to the air conditioning. There were no windows. She never knew whether it was warm or cold outside or when it got dark. As a result she walked slowly through the office, spoke to no one, held her head down.

The world shrank. It was defined by tiny operations - the pressing of a computer key - which too seconds rather than minutes, so that although th world was confined to a narrow space - her desk, t terminal, a few feet of carpet to pace towards the e of the day when there were few people in the office; the physical plane the world had shrunk to minute pr portions; but in the sense of time the universe co stantly expanded. She had not realised how long second could endure, or how pitifully quickly a action (blowing her nose, pulling up her socks) could be completed, when pitted against the thousands of seconds which mounted up each day. She timed herself, taught herself to breathe more slowly, wondered if eventually her heart would beat more slowly.

These rituals helped mark out

the
day: when she clocked
in each morning, she sat at her
desk and worked out the exact time she
could leave that evening: eight hours and
twelve minutes later. At regular fifteen minute
intervals she would recalculate how long was left
until the end of the day and make a note on a small pad
of paper beside her, crossing off the previous entry. As the
hours and minutes dwindled, especially after lunchtime, her
excitement rose, until in the last hour she would check the
time every couple of minutes. Approximately once an hour she
would leave her desk and walk slowly along the corridor to the
ladies' toilets, where she would sit on the toilet, fold her arms
across her stomach and rest her head on her knees for several
minutes. In an effort to warm herself she would then run hot
water over the backs of her hands and dry them under the hot
air dryer.

At ten o'clock, as the rest of the office crowded into the
corridor for the tea trolley, she would take a small packet
of raisins from her bag and eat them slowly one by one,
one raisin per computer transaction. In this way she
prolonged the tiny oral gratification she received
from the raisins (their sharp sweetness, and
the enjoyment of mastication), and she
slowed down the process of her
work to the minimum -
another

source
of gratification.
On a pad of paper she wrote
cryptic phrases charged with personal
significance in minute handwriting. She
could not write smaller, she had diminished,
shrunk down her writing to the utmost, and she
wished to accomplish the same effect with her presence. After re-reading and absorbing the impact of
each text she would then obliterate it with thick blocks
of black ink until the sheet of paper was covered in dense
black squares and she would screw it up and throw it in
the bin. This was her only means of subversion.
Her day seemed to be filled with numbers: the time the
alarm went off in the morning (6.32), the time she clocked
in for work and the time she clocked out, the combina-
tion lock on her bicycle (2642), her PIN number, all the
figures and dates and reference numbers she tapped
in on the computer. Often when she was cycling
home she would find herself repeating figures
from work over and over in her head, or
she would notice a number plate and
an insidious rhythm would
begin: F169 FGX, F169
F G X .

At
work, the time she
could leave sat in huge fat
figures inside her head: 16.55.
She hated numbers: they were
restricting, impersonal, the whole substance of work. Words were her one solace.
For her, words held a secret power, this was a
world no one else could enter. It gave her
power to hide code words on the computer:
REVOLT, UNITY, CHAOS. It pleased her to come
across these personal slogans, to know these words
were festering, breathing, infiltrating inside the
computer, slowly subverting the authority of figures. She thought of them as incendiary devices,
unpredictable and volatile, which would one day
explode.
Work words were of course necessarily dead.
The password she had been given for the computer epitomised their attitude: TASK. It
was such an ugly word. A school word. If
she had been able to choose her own
password she would have chosen
a word full of resonance, a
word to enjoy using
e a c h

day,
feeling the shape of the
word in her mouth, mulling over
its texture and secret meanings, content in the knowledge that it was embedded
in the computer, slowly hatching like a cancer.
She wondered why she had taken this job, why she
stayed, but she could not leave. The building impris-
oned her, with its time clock, its windowless rooms, its
continuous, pacifying air conditioning hum. The time
showed in the right hand corner of her terminal, so that
she could have counted every minute, every second of her
day, if she had wanted to, if she had been able to bear to.
With each day her world grew smaller; she invented dozens
of strategies to avoid having to visit other areas of the
office. She went upstairs rarely, upstairs where there
were windows, people who knew her.
Sitting at her desk she would bend lower over her terminal, shielding her face with her hand, hunching over
the small pad of paper as she wrote and
destroyed, wrote and destroyed, waiting for
that glorious moment when the nanobombs
she had planted would go off, melting
the screens, crumbling the
tyranny of numbers.

scat

darren francis

a novel extract

1.

Alex stands by the open window. Skin as washed out as faded photographs. Barely eighteen, shoulder-length hair, half-erect penis, laughter. Slivers of plaster pepper his arms, disappear like snow upon snow. Acid smell of semen.

Alex walks across the room, flaccid now, hands on buttocks.

Stoops, takes a chicken wishbone from the floor, hooks a little finger through each strand, pulls it in two and remembers Christian.

Dirty fingernails. Minute flakes of excrement. Alex blinks. Looks up at the ceiling. Sits on the bed, pink sheets folded like labia around his transparent body.

2.

I'm standing in the room next door to Alex, door closed between us. Earth spins below me. Time turns light around.

Dusk.

Nirvana Foster sat by the window in half-lotus. My bare feet silent on Chianti-coloured carpet, treading the rhythm of her breaths. Sweat bead poised on her brow like a patient Buddha. A jade elephant hangs between her breasts, two rings through her left nipple and one through the right. Dyed blonde hair with many extensions; red, yellow, blue, green, orange and black serpents that touch the small of her back. Breasts newspaper white, unlike the steady tan across the rest of her body that stops short at a line around her waist, becomes a cream triangle upon her shaven pubis.

A Trabant pulls up outside. Men in black suits essay out, cross over to another doorway. Nirvana opens her eyes. The sweat breaks free of her brow and down her cheek. Nirvana is not her real name, of course. One day someone will tell her that Nirvana is what you become, not what you are. I ask her,

'was it good?'

'Better than your snide remarks.'

'I wasn't being snide. Besides, you seem to do it so much.'

'Not so much.'

'How much is not so much?'

'I meditate for exactly twenty-three minutes twice a day; once at seven thirty and again at nineteen thirty.'

'But why? What's the point?'

'Enlightenment. It's all a question of discipline. Master discipline, and the rest falls into place on its own.'

'But do you always have to do it naked?'

'Of course I do. Clothing disrupts the flow of energy across the body.'

The mischievous flash of a polaroid; Alex stands in the doorway in stained grey jeans, camera to eye. Nirvana jumps up, chases him from the room in a flail of arms and breasts. Alex runs to the end of the hall, points the camera, clicks two more shots of naked Nirvana. Leaps into the air, Pandean. Nirvana fumes, stands with one hand on her hip and the other pointing into Alex's room.

'Get back in there, or I'll send you back to your mother!'

Alex turns on his heels, gasps:

'D-don't shout... it makes - makes you look ugly.'

Night. Nirvana and me in bed, Alex's camera boxed away, the upset over. Nirvana burns beside me, while Alex snores in the room next door and aircraft skim the skies.

Panic.

Christian storms cloven-hooved through Alex's sleep and dreams become churning horses, send Alex tossing hard into the sheets. Soak his skin, tangle his hair. Dawn and Alex awake, but the tangles won't let themselves be removed. Nirvana gives hours, stands behind Alex and yanks a brush through his hair.

'Ouch! Ouch! Fuck! Hurts!'

Alex flails his arms like a burn victim, like he's going to hit Nirvana but he doesn't. Nirvana stops, waits until Alex's hands return to his knees, then resumes her tugging.

'This can't go on' Nirvana says. 'I'm sick of you and your damn dreams and photos, Alex. Why can't you be like you used to be?'

3.

Hazy Sunday.

I sleep through the afternoon, through the incessant drone of

Nam myoho renge kyo nam myoho renge kyo nam myoho renge kyo nam myoho renge kyo nam myoho renge kyo nam myoho renge kyo nam myoho renge kyo nam myoho renge kyo nam myoho renge kyo nam myoho renge kyo nam myoho renge kyo nam myoho renge kyo nam myoho renge kyo nam myoho renge kyo nam

myoho renge
kyo nam
myoho renge
kyo nam
myoho renge
kyo nam
myoho renge
kyo nam
myoho renge
kyo nam
myoho renge

kyo nam myoho renge kyo nam myoho renge kyo nam myoho renge kyo nam myoho renge kyo...'
because sometimes Nirvana forgets her tight routine to Satori, and her meditations ramble for hours. So I sleep. Christian fills my slumber, as if dreams of him were a contagious disease.

Christian dances in a shower of gold.

Prowls public lavatories, taking photographs and making notes and turning slim wrists in his hands. We slugger through Hyde Park, day departing in a golden shower of sun.

It was through Christian that I learned of what he terms *The Alchemy Of The Anus*. Christian crafts excrement, not purely with hands but with a chemisty of words, knows that to the subconscious brain gold and excrement are interchangeable.

'*A psychoanalyst, knowing that gold and excrement are akin in the subconscious, would not have been surprised that I used my shit - like the droppings of the Golden Ass, or Danae's divine diarrhoea - to perform a phenomenal transmutation through the application of my paranoia-critical method...*

'Dali. It's alchemy. I'm preparing a book, a metaphysical study entitled *The Alchemy Of The Anus*. Dali calls it *The Humanism Of The Arsehole*, of course, but I have no interest in crudity. The most potent orgasms I have experienced have been anal. Primarily solo. No, I'm being modest there, but solo is where the most studious experiments may be staged.

'Something was needed to slake my appetite for miracles. I began to substitute fingers with a variety of household objects - the obvious banana or cucumber, hair brush, tooth brush, deodorant can, pencil - the mundane became a vital part of my bliss. And that is alchemy. Everyday items tucked down the staircase. Perfect from mundane, energy from action, gold from excrement. Manson found a hole in the desert, covered it up, named it the Devil's Hole. Knew that when the end was here, Helter Skelter coming down fast, he and his chosen family would shelter there.'

Christian's words glimmer like diamanté. Forbidden and obsessive. Yet I get what Christian proffers and nothing more. To approach Christian for answers is to solicit an insidious smile and a finger fixed firmly to lips. Horus, Crowned and Conquering Child and Lord of the Aeon, straddling the gateway to silence and secrecy.

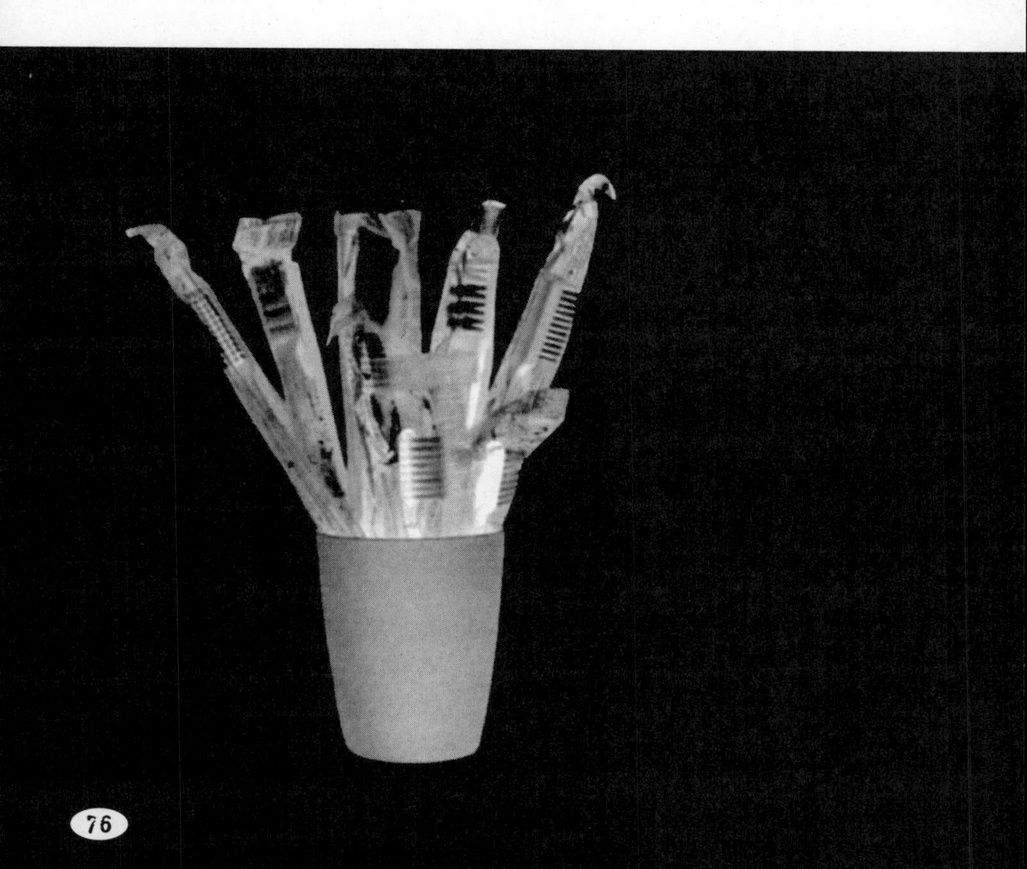

performance death

penny j cotton

He's taken tougher knocks, has Ed. He knows it's on the cards. It came up just yesterday, just casually. Oh, Ed, I said. The low life has lost its appeal. Cash on the nail is just a fairy tale and I don't believe in magic any more. And he laughed his multi–edged survivor's laugh, full of hardness and tears and things which don't have words.

I decided for sure somewhere between midnight and dawn. I got up when the light got grainy, and now I'm sitting and staring at the outside. It's raining. The pigeons shelter on my window ledge. They shake the water from their wings, their concrete and sludge and paving slab wings. The down on their heads sticks up like gelled quiffs. I warm to them, the plebiscites of the bird world, the scavengers.

Opposite me is a tower block, the twin of the one I live in. It reminds me of the worst type of person: arrogant, though it lacks everything except a function. But it's not so bad. It was built in the '50s, when the art of the eyesore was still in its infancy; but at least it's built of bricks, and at least there are only seven stories.

Ed's is worse by far. A million miles high, smog-coloured, slashed with concrete byways. How can you stand it, I said when I first saw it. I live in the wreckage of someone's dream, he said, ...it's poetry. You live in someone's fuck-up, I told him. You, he said, have no sense of the poignant. I think I spat, but I kept the saliva out of it, because Ed makes me laugh.

Ed thinks everything in life is poetry, or theatre, or a performed poem. I think he got the idea from long-dead literary types. But he really lives it, and in his own bitter way, and in that he's original. He doesn't just find poetry in the banal; he finds it in the supremely disgusting. I once saw him stare for an hour at a dog turd in Vauxhall. The shit so soft, so organic; the pavement so implacable, so inanimate. I looked at it for a while, too. They eat all this stuff from tins, I said, and it comes out of their bums looking exactly the same. For a moment I was rapt.

He'll survive this. But he'll be pissed off. He has a hard time finding lovers. For one thing, he never goes out, and most of his clients are men. But mainly, he looks so fucked he should be dead. The cadaverous aesthetic, he said proudly, when I pointed it out. It's the legacy of time and twenty-three hour days and smack. Especially smack. It accelerates the aging process. His photograph should be posted up in schools to deflect wannabe addicts: Hey, babes, this is where you're heading.

I knew how things might pan out when I got offered the job. I've looked for jobs before. Ed could never understand why. He worked once, in a box office at a theatre. He stuck it as long as I stuck the Brownies: about two hours. We've chatted about work. He talks a lot of shit, Ed, but sometimes he'll say something lucid, and it'll claw through my mind, keep coming back just when I don't want it. Work will make you mediocre, he said. Nothing wrong with that, I said tetchily. If people didn't conform, society would collapse. Other people do it naturally, he said. Not you. You'd have to make a big effort. There was no one else in the flat at the time, but he peered intensely around the room. He likes acting paranoid. He leaned over, his pale eyes almost lost in his squint. He said, the bits that don't fit are the bits that count. But it's pretty uncomfortable, being the wrong shape.

I know when it's full-blown morning, because the air outside is less porridgey and because my neighbour puts her Elvis Presley tape on full. I've never met her, but I know a bit about her, the scrawny walls have seen to that. I know about her love for Elvis, about her deafness, about her insomnia and her bad chest. I know I need to retaliate. I turn my Beethoven tape over in my hands then set it aside. He's the wrong guest for my cracked and crusty bedsit. I invite REM instead, and they blend in perfectly.

I am expected at Ed's at two, and I'm always on time. It'll all be for the best. He's better off alone. And I'll be gentle. Ed, I'll say. I'm not dumping you. I'm setting you free. It's poetry.

I wore a skirt and tights and cuban heels, to show him I was serious. I wore no make up, so I looked ill and piteous and not anger-inducing. I strode all the way, purposefully, pausing only to toss a coin at a nomadic trumpet player. You walk strong, said the trumpet player. I like that.

The sight of the estate sapped away some of that strength. It was a brutal scar against a scarred sky; it was a gruesome lesson in perspective. And the lift was crazy with graffiti and out of order, so I climbed up the stinking piss-drenched stairs. I gasped for breath as I laboured upwards. It'll get worse, I thought, with my job. Office work.

Sedentary. But it won't matter because of the salary. Mine was a future free of tower blocks, where piss would always end up in toilets.

I reached the right floor. I stood for a few seconds, bent over, catching my breath. My legs trembled. I stood up straight. I turned wearily around. And I saw Ed's door, bleached, graunched, flung open, blocking the passageway.

My heart, just calming down now I'd reached level ground, sped back into overdrive. I walked slowly, inevitably, warily. I could hear voices. Loud, official. Oh my god, I thought. He's been busted. I should flee, they'll take me for a punter. But I'm not clued up, I'm not canny, I always fall to bits in times of crisis. I lurched forward as though shoved from behind; I hoped the cuban heels would get me off the hook.

It's the pigs, alright. A whole mob of them. I stand uselessly on the doorstep. I hear kerfuffle. A female sees me, walks over, blocks entrance. I know she's female because her lower half is boxed into a rhombus-shaped skirt.
–Can I help you? says she.
–I've come to see my mate, say I.
–This his place, is it? says she.
I nod, I shake my head, I nod, I pretend to be doing an impromptu neck exercise. You are playing straight into their hands, I tell myself. Then I look beyond her shoulder. I can see the bathroom. Its door is flung open. I see a blur of red. It's logical, that; all his walls are the colour of blood. But still. Something is badly wrong. I hear water splashing. Ed, I cry, and try to barge in.

The next thing I know, I'm trapped in the living room with the rhombus and her beefy boss. They smear a cosmetic called Sympathy over their faces, but all I can see is the prurient fascination underneath. From the hallway there is banging, there are voices, there is water splashing. This Ed's place is it? says Rhombus again. My mouth opens and shuts and opens. She can't talk English, says the beefy one. And then his sprawling face is inches from mine, and he is yelling at me, putting big gaps between his words. What's his surname, what comes after Edward. Ed is not from the beginning of Edward, I say in my best accent, but from the middle of Frederick. It's a well-rehearsed sentence, for people often make this mistake. It comes out fluently.

But the fluency left me. I began to babble. What's happening, What's going on, and making feeble lunges at the door. They sat me down on the ratty sofa. They'd got him in the nick of time, they said. Neighbour A saw Neighbour B breaking in through the window and called the police. Another few minutes, and old Ed, submerged in bath water, blood pumping from his arteries, would have been a goner. The ambulance had taken him away, and things were being

cleaned up. Maybe he would be saved. I looked at them both. No one had ever seemed so concerned about Ed's fate.

I noticed how tidy the living room was. All the dealing equipment, the scales, the bits and pieces wrapped in cling film, all gone. The stage was prepared. And my role had been to find the body in the bath. I glanced over at the bookcase, at the Yeats which concealed the hiding place where we left secrets for each other.

–Did he leave anything, say I to Rhombus, my voice hoarse and rusty. Did he leave a note?

–They usually do, says she. But we haven't found anything yet.

I glanced at the Yeats, then at my jailer. Water, I said. I need water.

Then I changed it to tea, which would take more time to make.

The letter was behind the Yeats. That, at least, went smoothly. I didn't read it till I staggered from his flat. I read it over and over as I wandered, blind to everything except his words. I'm tired of acting solo, he said, so I'm giving you the final act. Maybe you will revise your plot.

You botched it. It's unbelievable. For days I wandered, furious. You botched it because you weren't there to direct it, because the actors didn't get their scripts, because a rogue neighbour and a nosy neighbour could gatecrash the show and call the police too early, before you or I were ready. Because performance is not the same as life. You botched it so I never saw your body, so the fact of your death is a bald, solid lump outside of me, which I keep trying to grab and chew and digest. But when, for a second, I can hold it, it breaks my teeth; when I can swallow it, my gut contracts and spews it back up.

For days I wandered. I ended up on Hampstead Heath. At nights I watched the boys with each other. They didn't notice me, or they didn't care. By day, there were the walkers and the skaters, and the kite flyers, made less sweet and simple because of the luminous outfits, because of the nylon plumes which roared as they soared. My mind full of my Ed's voice and my voice and Ed's. You think the whole of life is a performance, Ed. You live on a cloud. It's not a cloud, Ed said. It's the last resort. And perhaps, as I wandered, perhaps, through my fury, I began to understand a few more things. I found more words for that laugh of his, which was manic and knowing, which was bleakly and brutally amused.

Rhombus came back with my cup of tea, looking suspicious. As I sipped it, she asked concerned, caring questions which ferreted about for information incognito. How long had I known Ed? Had we been close? What did he do for a living? That's right, I thought. Get me while I'm down. I crouched over, darkly, monosyllabic. It's gloomy in here, she said. Let's have a bit of light. And the heavy velvet curtains, eternally drawn, stiff as flutes through misuse, were shaken by the hand of Rhombus. I leapt up, panicking. Ed hated natural light. Even in England, even in drizzle, he wore dark glasses. He said it was crucial for the imagination.

They left me alone after that scene. I drank my tea and looked at the life-size photos of Ed in more beautiful days when his limbs were plump, his fingers slender, his skin peachy. Perhaps he kept them there to torture himself; perhaps to impress his clients. I looked at them because, out of everything in the room, they had the least to do with Ed.

They let me go, when my tea was gone. I had to give them my details and promise that we'd meet again. Then I fled. I ran as fast as I could from the wreckage of someone's dream.

On my hand is a cut, inflicted by Ed's talons about a fortnight ago, the day before The Day. Every so often, I stop what I'm doing to stare at it, conscious that soon it will heal without a trace, it will cease to exist.

He died. At least he got that bit right. But I'm not going to revise my plot. I'm packing my things, I'm moving out, I've got a job to do and a salary to be paid. And as I walk along pavements, I glance at boys in suits who have round faces, whose drugs are legal, who are the same age as me. And they glance back, because of the skirt and the tights and the cuban heels.

It's dawn. My bedsit is shorn. The walls are stripped, the clutter crammed into cardboard boxes. It's going to be hot, I can tell. I sit on the floor. It is very quiet. But an aeroplane packs the silence with its rumble. Then it starts. Love me tender, love me true, never let me go. For my darling I love you, and I always will. I am totally still. I move only enough to shift air through my lungs. My neighbour, not a rogue, not nosy, has stepped in for the final scene.

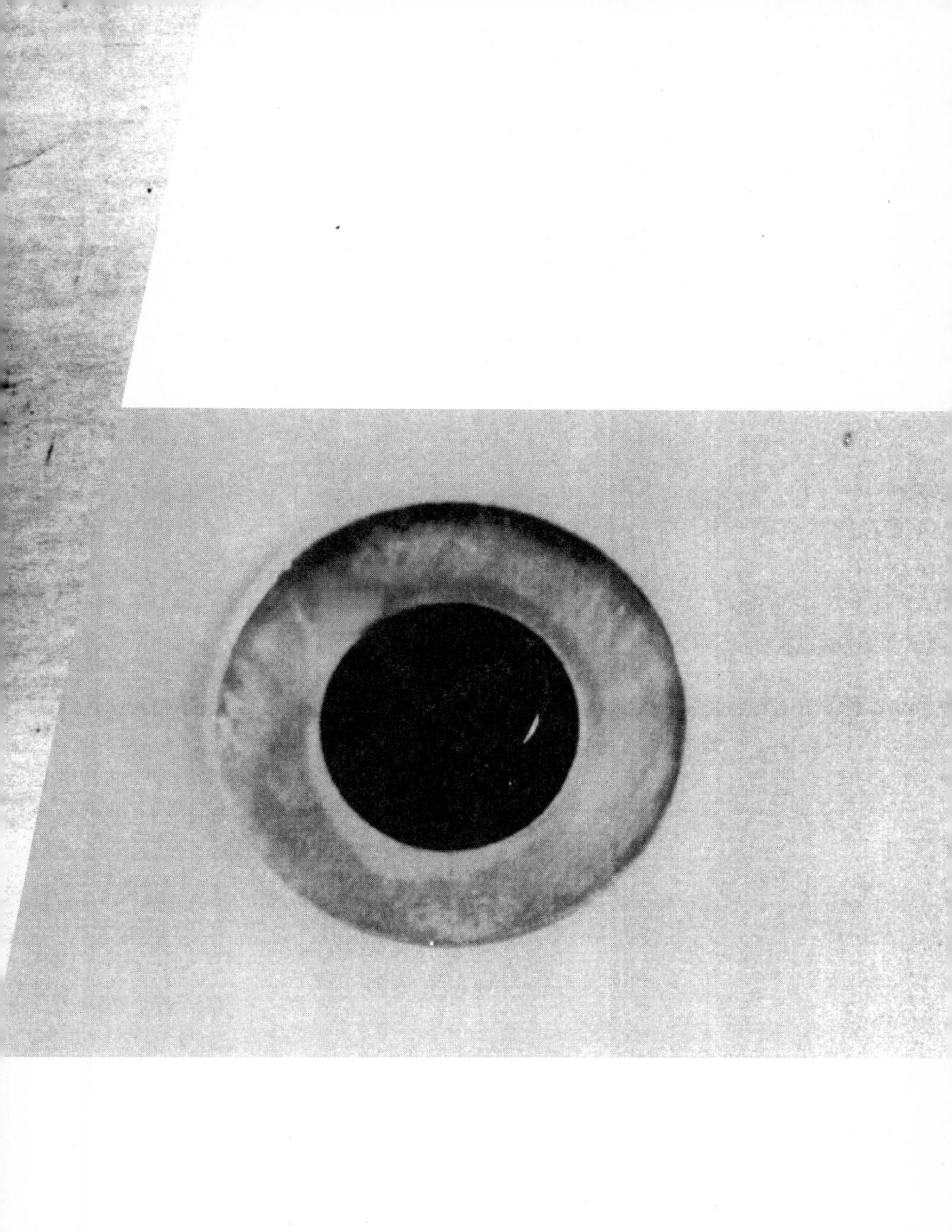

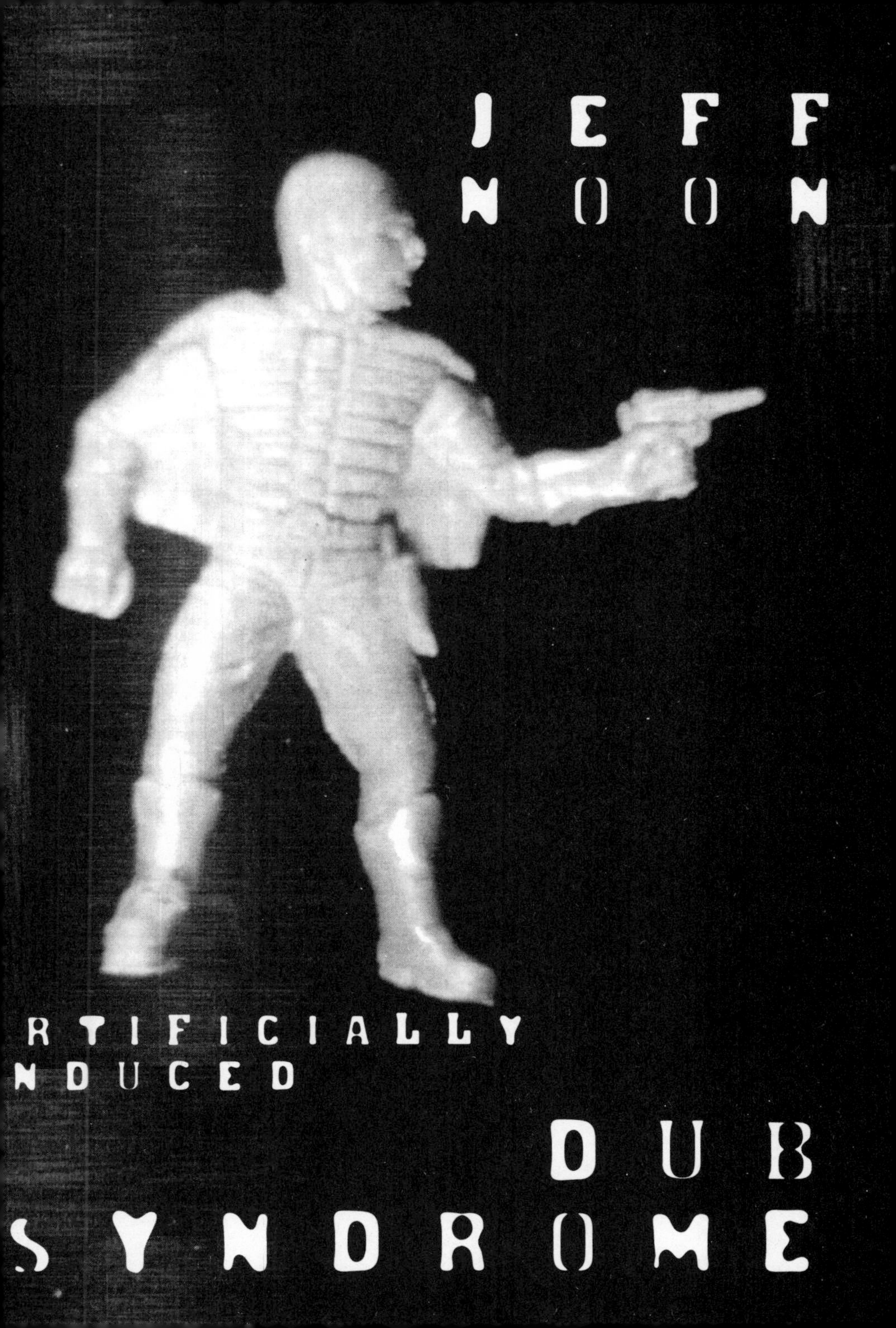

JEFF NOON

RTIFICIALLY
NDUCED

DUB
SYNDROME

Rising upwards from Manchester, England, sickening from the dislocation changes, sucking our way into the dream-space of Amirrorca, to land at the Donald Duck runway, five seconds later.

L i k e . . . u h h . . . w h o o o o s h , man!...Like...uhh...shit!...Where in the head am I?...Captain can you help me, please?

"We hope you all enjoyed the trip, and please fly with World Psyche again, y'hear? We sure do appreciate your custom."

And then the mad scramble for the exit node. Into Neutral.

This was mine and Jodie's first ever trip to the UD of A, so you can guess we were suffering. I was getting my head round it, you know, second by second, if only to impress Krunch, but poor Jodie...man, she was screaming down the Art Deco corridors. Chillingly good interface, by the way; these Americans really knew how to make a dream live. I mean, the place looked more than real. Maybe this is why Jodie was suffering so; she was used to the old English Fantasy, with it's cheap and nasty "Singland welcomes careful dreamers" design, where all the edges are fuzzy and the people feel like warmed-up cheese. Still, the girl wasn't helping our mission any, waving her arms around like that, and shouting abuse at the other refugees as they streamed through Neutral, towards the border controls. A pack of splicehounds had now locked onto Jodie's manic scent; I could hear them snarling and pounding their cages, eager to rip flesh from some errant smuggler.

Okay, the UDA Immigration Authorities had splicehounds on their side; we had Krunch-Factor 9 on ours. The big Dogman slapped Jodie around the face, once or twice — claws sheathed, naturally — and then pushed her towards the customs post. She ran a smoky pathway between the sniffer beams of the splicers and the icy stares of the loaded guardsmen. No fire-sirens. Krunch himself cleared the customs like a well-heeled business-exec, firmly on his hind legs for the disguise. Now the pair of them are staring at me from the safe side of the dream. Nice of them that, considering that I was the cargo-carrier! One false move passing through the barrier, I was spliced-up meat and gravy on a pair of slobbering jaws. Man, this was gonna be one dangerous gig.

Let me introduce the band...

Jodie Ace was the singer and the lyricist. One gorgeous half-cast shadow of a girl, a little strung-up on being down, but with a voice of dewy mist, I swear, and a pair of smoky eyes that could read the contents of your mind from the distance of a kiss. And then turn all your secrets into a song...

I made a step towards the barrier that marked the end of Neutrality. Beyond that point, Amirrorca. Freedom's dance. The splicehounds started to growl.

Jodie was the song and I was the music, with the buzz-name of Lemon Deuce. I could turn myself into the drums and the violin, the acoustic and electric guitars, the piano and the trumpet, the ocarina and the Tibetan nose flute; shit, man, I could turn my body into anything that made a noise, but best of all I liked to turn myself into the double bass. This was my Mingus Demon, my deep down throb of bliss. Yeah, I was a Dub sufferer. I had the music virus swimming my cells. What else could I do with my illness, but allow some of its symptoms to add rhythm and lead to Jodie's soulfulness? We called our business Ace and the Deuce, purveyors of the finest illegal dance music.

Another step forwards. I was almost level with the first splicehound now. The rabid beast was making a thick bass grumble, like he'd sniffed out the aroma of Mingus on my skin. Stay cool. One of the borderguards had his hand ready on the cage release. Don't look at the guard! Look forwards. There's Krunch, just a few small steps away. He's waiting for me in Amirrorca. The bastard's grinning at me!

Krunch-Factor 9 was the wild card in the hand, our latest management. Krunch was halfdog and halfman, but with the dog-half in denial, full to the shaved-off cheek-fur with promises of mega-dosh. On a good day he could almost pass for human.

All those promises that I'd followed, upwards and dreamwards, downwards and along, across the line, between the sights of robodogs and marksmen. Another step forwards. Any second now, expecting the sirens to start, the jaws to shut, the bullets to explode...

Krunch hired a Mustang Detonate from the dreamport's courtesy counter, and within fifteen minutes we were speeding away from Newer York City, northwards, through a neat array of suburbs. I was in the back with Jodie, trying my best to calm her down. Krunch was upfront and driving. Outside, the American Dream flashed by like a series of movie sets; a kid on a bike throwing newspapers onto front porches, an old soldier manicuring his lawn, a young golf-widow pushing the dog and walking the pram. And take a look at that giant, yellow W! Shit, the Americans couldn't even dream unless it contained burgers! The burbs petered out into a mess of shanty towns, where scrawny youths chased after a screaming piglet. The dream getting nastier. Some ruffian banged on the Mustang's window as we nudged around a pile of dream-trash. Krunch gave him the old canine one claw gesture and then accelerated; I could hear the kid screaming as we shot out of the sprawl. Open country. Sparse was the traffic, likewise the conversation. I was still seething from the gauntlet. "Play us some tune, Lemon Boy," Krunch finally growled at me. Canine and English.

"What about the cops?" I asked.

"You be seeing Boogie Cops, yes?" Krunch snarled. "Me not seeing no cops. Not at all! Road belongs to the swift."

"You didn't exactly help, Krunch, back there at the border."

"You not need any help."

"You helped Jodie."

"You got through good, no? Those cheap splicerhounds! Jesus Dog! Lemon Boy, your music be too deeply ridden for finding. Come on! Me thinking Jodie want to sing, yes? Calm her down some?"

From the look of her, the last thing on Jodie's mind was singing. She was pressing herself into the upholstery, sweat pouring from her brow. What else could I do but start some viral bass and drums in my veins? Mingus Demon and the Moon Demon, making my weak, thin body emit a dubbed-up version of Bass Spacer. It needed Jodie's sweet and smoking vocals, but the shadowgirl kept her mouth and her mind closed.

Krunch was tapping out the rhythm on the steering wheel, howling along quite tunelessly, until a honking siren added its treble pitch to my body's bass, and then Jodie started on a wailing scream.

Boogie Cops! Keepers of the Stillness. Man, those bastards were sure nimble for danceophobes!

The Authorities were scared of rhythm, you see, like they were scared of sex between the species. Man, those Authorities were neuters; they were scared of their own dried-up apertures! The brain-dead nano-fucks! Which is a laugh, because the Authorities were all for Vurt in the early days. Vurt was the name of an organic technology that allowed humans to walk, as though real, through the landscape of dreams. Above the real world called England, the Authorities created a vurtual world called United Singland; above the real world called America, a vurtual world called the United Dreams of Amirrorca. The various dreams eventually joined hands, and all around the surface of Planet Earth floated Planet Vurt. Lots of Earthlings actually wanted to become Vurtlings; they wanted to live in their dreams forever. Access was strictly controlled, of course, via tollbooths and border controls, and a rising scale of fares; the deeper the dream, the higher the price. The Authorities were cleaning up! Until it all started to go wrong, and the dream-disease imported itself into reality.

It started in Manchester, of course, the thinnest membrane. You can imagine the Town Hall's despair as the first cases of Dub Sickness came to light. They'd always had a limp dick for music anyway, what with its "liberating effect upon the young", but this was a square's nightmare, because music was now a viral intruder. I mean, music was actually penetrating the people. Seven per cent of the World's population were infected. And you're listening to the story of one of the first. We had all these demon players inside us, virus musicians from heaven that we could call up at anytime. Jesus Jagger, those early days...did we make the people dance, or what?! Even worse for the Authorities, the fact that the Dub virus could be passed on through sex. They called it the new VD for propaganda purposes. (Vurtual Dynamics, don't you know?)

Against a disease from an unknown dream, what chance of a cure? All the Authorities managed was to introduce the Laws of Stillness, a vicious edict that ruled against the pursuit of moving your body (in Reality or Vurtuality) to the measures of a repetitive beat; the Laws of Purity, which outlawed sex with a sufferer; and the Laws of Quarantine, a rather sweet name for the rounding up and imprisonment of all known sufferers. And one by one the nations fell, until this time that I'm telling about, when the Earth and its dream became quite unmoving and morose.To administer these pathetic measures, pray welcome the Stillness Enforcement League. To outlaw dancers the world and the dream over, otherwise known as the Boogie Cops...

I closed down the Mingus and the Moon demons, as a cop-car pulled us over to the road's edge. Two seconds later, a Boogie she-cop was banging on the driver's window. "Is anything the matter, officeress?" Krunch politely asked, with an immaculate human voice, all of a sudden. Man, that Krunch could play any game!

"The matter," the Boogie Cop replied, "is that we've picked up some illegal bass and drums being played on the dreamway."

"Officeress, does it look like we've got a drum kit in the vehicle? We have no interest in music. Unless it be the kind produced by rubbing your back legs together."

"Listen, bud...I've had a bad day."

"Please, we're an innocent trio of Mancunian enginemologists, heading on to Connect'n'cut for a convention on the mating habits of the robo-beetle. These remarkable creatures attract partners by rubbing their back legs together, thus producing a lusty, melodious song. Here are our papers...I think you'll find them all in order."

"What's wrong with her?" The Boogie Cop was looking at Jodie.

"She's dream-lagged from the flight," Krunch replied, cool as dog-fuck.

The cop gazed at Jodie for a full ten seconds, then turned back to Krunch: "You wouldn't be a dogman, by any chance?"

"Officeress, please! How dare you? Dogmen are the scum of rabid DNA. I just haven't had a shave for a few weeks. That's all."

"Well...in Connect'n'cut..."

"Yes?"

"I recommend you buy some shaving tablets."

And then we were free, and riding. Open country. Krunch Factor 9 coming up trumps against one easy Boogie Cop! Maybe this trip wasn't such a bad idea, after all. Even Jodie seemed to be more at ease: she'd stopped shaking by now, and looking down at her shadowy face, I even caught a trace of love being stroked through my mind.

Or maybe not, as the case may be...

Things had never been easy between us. It wasn't just musical differences, (although Jodie's insistence upon me releasing ancient Motown Demons sometimes riled); neither was it the singer against the band, because I was happy up in the DJ box — the last thing I needed was fame, what with the Boogies after my blood. It wasn't even that her Shadow allowed her access to my vilest thoughts...

Let me tell the truth...

After the Dubness invaded, I went right off women. I know some of the sufferers rejoiced in spreading the virus; they called it turning the world into music, pure music. But I was reticent and confused. Maybe I had an inkling about what the Dub would lead to, even then. I was gigging at a club called Jungle Jingles, a dingy hole in Unchester, Singland. Sure it was against the law, but the Boogies had a hard time policing the labyrinthine backstreets of Singland. Listen good: if the people want to dance, the people shall dance. Here and there in the dream you could find these tawdry palaces, whose managers were keen on the outlaw-dosh. After the gig, this young girl barged her way into the dressing room. I wasn't used to being harangued, the truth be known. "I suppose you're after my rhythm patterns?" My innocent question, to which the girl whispered in a breath of smoke, "I'm after your sperm."

It felt like my mind was being caressed by the fingers of a shadow.

That night I ended up in her bed, and we made a kind of love, I suppose: Jodie wanted everything but I was playing it safe. Our kisses floated like thought bubbles above trails of smoke from her skin. And after the kisses, this girl called Jodie Ace sang a lonesome song to me. Despite the virus running in beats through my body, this was a new song, and a new loving song. I tried to play along with my internal rhythm, but the beats came out all wrong...until Jodie gathered every drift of smoke from the room, blowing this dark cloud into my head. All the thoughts of a sad, young, constantly-searching girl seeping through me, and then...

Shiver song!

I was playing along with a new beat, a liquid rhythm. A demon musician called up from my dying cells. "Did you like that, Lemon?" Jodie asked, "It's called You Are, You Are."

"Whose beautiful song is that?" I pleaded.

"It's your song now, but originally Curtis sang it."

"Ian Curtis? The Joyful Divisionist?"

"Curtis Mayfield, silly! You call yourself a sufferer, but you've never played the Mayfield Demon before?"

"How did you do that new song to me?"

"Oh, you know...a little touch of Shadow. I just worked something loose for you. Now, won't you please give me the gift?"

Jodie really wanted to tune into the music direct, that constant searching, but still I refused to go all the way. For some slippery reason, I didn't want to reproduce the dream. Here, truly, begins the uneasiness between us.

But that was the origin of Ace and the Deuce, the smoke and dub of outlaw dance. And up and down the imagined Singland, again and again Ace and the Deuce fed the secret beat to eager, wet minds, making the people madly dance, making a secret joy in the darkness. Jodie and I, we made a dance of our own after the gigs, falling in love with each other and the illegal nature of our crimes against stillness. It was a chaste love, of course, and sometimes Jodie would scream at me, for denying her the ultimate access to music. But I was strong, I was safely-sexual. The intuitive knowledge inside, that this internal music would kill the sufferer eventually.

But how I loved those early days of our career, plying our illegal wares, easily finding a bass-path to dub out the cops. We were always on the run, of course; always only one small dancing step ahead of the Boogie Cops, but this escaping only fuelled my desire. Ace and the Deuce released a record called Bass Spacer, a dream the lawbreakers could swallow with pride.

Man, how they swallowed! That debut tune made it to number five in the outlaw charts and we were on some kind of dangerous roll I guess, because this is when Krunch-Factor 9 came visiting. We were playing the DFEX club in Unchester. Jodie was down on the imaginary stage, singing her soul out:—

Stop your running of the human race,
Lick your lips at the cut and paste.
Make a Curtis Mayfield kind of pace;
Leave some space for the bass.

This is when I made my human-bass solo, up in the DJ booth, feeding multiple dream-beats to the dancers. Ultra-low frequencies seeping out of my brain-amp. I called up the demon viruses of Mingus and Moon and Davis and Hendrix. And a little touch of Mayfield, just to please the singer. I was feeling like the Dreamiest Jockey of all-time, and the crowd was revelling in this trancing output of my body, dancing fit to burst against the laws. This is when Krunch-Factor 9 burst into the booth, in such a hurry that his sleeked-down whiskers sprung into life on his shaven cheeks.

"You the buzz, my friend!" he snarled above the music. "You be suffering from the dub-sickness, yes?"

"Yeah, I suffer..." Hesitant, you know, but I could tell that the dogman had sniffed out with his wet nose that I was plugged in direct to the music.

"Maybe I squeeze some mega-dosh out of you, yes?" Krunch was gazing down at Jodie's lovely shape on the stage as he growled this out. "You like this idea, Mister DJ Boy?"

Well, I wasn't too sure, but the next morning Jodie and I met up with the Dogman over a Full English Breakfast at the Cafe de Mush. Whilst dribbling bacon fat down his chin he regaled us with stories of "certain sub-dreams" within the United Dreamscape of America, and how they were "dancing ultra-good" over there: "They be dancing free!"

Jodie was dead set against it at first, mainly because of her Shadow's natural hatred of the Dogs.

"Me not no dog!" Krunch whimpered in response: "Me a man. Me pure." Smoothing his cut-to-the-quick claws along his cheeks the same time, pathetically hoping to hide the stubble of his fur.

"They kill you for dancing in Amirrorca," Jodie said. "Everybody knows that."

"Everybody forgetting the Originals, yes?" Krunch replied: "The Original Peoples of Amirrorca, they be one autonomous zone. They make the dancing free and easy. Big dosh! Mega Dosh! Why, they let Dub sufferers play free in that zone. Originals love the sufferers! You two following me?"

Following...

Upwards and dreamwards and downwards and along, until we were driving through the snow-layered forests of Connect'n'cut, a sparse realm of lonely log-cabins and broken-down tractors. The further we got from Newer York City, the fuzzier the interface became. Until the trees were shedding leaves like fragments of information. We turned one final, icy bend in the Mustang. The Original's borderline was just ahead of us, and beyond its shimmering curtain of frosty air the forest disappeared into mist. Maybe Jodie started to feel at home then, I don't know, but her shadow was quivering with a new love for that smokiness beyond the borderline. I was feeling my bass notes throb.

"Almost home, my people!" Krunch announced with a bark, like he was howling down all the laws of stillness. "Fucking dosh-bound!"

Maybe we could, at last, make this dream come true?

A bunch of people were gathered around the entry point, brandishing placards and shouting out fiery slogans: Originals go home! Vurth belongs to Earth! No more Unreservations! Kill the Twindians dead! Stop the evil rhythm! No more dancing! No more music disease! That stupid kind of stuff.

Jodie started to whimper over the shadow between us: Krunch unsheathed his claws to full-on mastiff mode.

Maybe not such an easy dream...

Can you Imagine America's surprise when it first ventured into the dreamworld of Amirrorca; to find a people already living in the Vurt? America thought it was uncovering an untold continent; in fact it was invading a homeland. These natives of the dream called themselves the Original People. America called them the Red Twindians, and declared war on them, repeating the history of oppression. Until it was discovered that the Originals actually controlled access to the dreamworld; without the Originals, America could not dream. America had to compromise. The Originals were allowed to remain in their

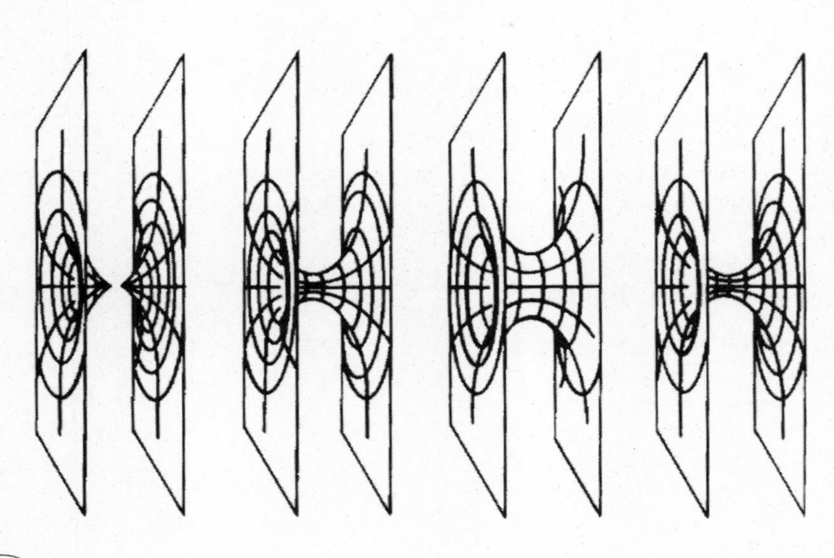

homeland, but only within a few autonomous zones, known as the Unreservations. Of course the Originals used this autonomy to their own advantage, granting passage to all the desires that America deemed criminal, of which there were plenty, but dancing to repetitive music was the worst. America was shit-scared of the dancing virus. All the bad things came to be associated with Original Amirrorca. Which made for bad-ass press.

Krunch was now forcing a pathway through the protesters, waving his sharpened dog-claws around like a wicked promise. I was doing my best to keep up with him, dragged down as I was with Jodie's newly-awakened reluctance, and the scrabbling blows of the protest line. "Traitor to Earth!" one of them called me. "Twindian lover! Traitor, traitor, traitor!" I pulled Jodie along through the storm, reaching Krunch at the gateway. The Dogman was arguing with the border guard, demanding free passage to the Unreservation. The guard was shaking his heavy head and slow-speaking in alien syllables. "Me not make snout nor tale of this talking," the Krunch barked, total-dog. "What you hearing, Deuce Boy?"

This was the first Original I had ever seen, and his crimson skin and his yellow eyes, and the array of silvery feathers tied to his long, midnight blue hair...these attributes burned a hole in my soul. I couldn't explain why.

"I'm hearing patterns, Krunch..."

"Deuce baby, you be playing some tune to him, yes?"

All around I could hear the traitor-calls, but still, I played...

I called up some ancient demons; I called up the drumming virus from Afreaka, and the Cajun virus from Loose'n'easiana; I even called up the reggae bass virus from old Jam-maker. I dug deep down, to play a primal tune. The Original cracked his deep creases into the semblance of a smile, and then plucked one of the silvery feathers from his hair. He offered it to me. I didn't know what to do. "Him wanting you to swallow it," Krunch whispered.

So I swallowed, and so did Jodie and the Krunch; each of us, in turn, tickling the back of our throats with the offering feather.

And then dissolving...through the gateway to danceland...

Three hours later, man, I'm telling you. A multiverse of terpsichorians were outlaw-pounding the snows of dreamland into slush. Jodie was down on the stage between the

Tumtum trees, singing with such beauty that even the Jubjub birds in the branches were beating their wings in time. And, for the very first time, I was on stage with the singer, playing the instruments of my sickness. I was free at last, to express my love. A kiss from my cells, and the people were dancing; Dub was welcomed here. I felt strong and viral, strong and virile, even. Especially when Bass Spacer came on-line. I turned the dream into joy-flesh and wantonness.

Five hours later, all but danced-out and glimmering, my brain's amp-lights turned to embers, I'm ready for my bed. I'm ready, at last and fuelled-up; enough dancing lust within me to want to pass on the Dub virus. But Jodie wasn't there. Jodie wasn't in my bed. I walk along pastel corridors. Another hotel door. Jodie wasn't there. Another bad dream. Jodie wasn't there. Another wisp of smoke. Another door. And there I find my once upon a time beauty, pouring her misty body all over Krunch's bristling fur.

Jesus of the Dream, how far have I got to go?

I make my lonely way towards my bedroom. I fall into a troubled sleep, into which a scarlet native comes ranting. The moniker is Moonkeeper. I'm the dumbfuck drummer of the tribe. You played well, tonight, my mate. Take this feather as your payment.

Taking a silvery, scarlet feather from the greasy braids of a chief.

Let me show you the sights...

Following the Original down into a deeper land, a dream within a dream, where dancing was nothing unnatural, where dancing was gold. Moonkeeper telling me that he used to be called Keep Moon, in the real world, raging drummer with The Whom. (I think he was losing the plot a little.) And that Keep Moon had died ages and ages ago, and that his dreaming soul had been reborn to this Vurtdom called Beat Heaven. "So this is how the Moon Demon managed to get inside my cells?" I asked. My mate, I fed my drums into your body, the native replied. We wanted to get back to Earth, natch. We wanted to party again. Yeah, we're your disease and proud of it. How come you're not into shagging? Shagging's beautiful. Don't you want to pass on the gift? Can't you understand our yearning?

Of course I understand; Beat Heaven...the dream of drumming...

I saw Hendrix there, playing with bright fire; I saw Joplin and Morrison there, singing with blue flowers. It was like the cheapest hippy death-dream, until I saw

Curtis and Holly and Miller, making music out of forgiveness. I saw Mingus thrumming at the triple bass. I saw the Moon, and the Moon was pounding on the skin of the sky...

And then awakening. My corrugated face in a hotel mirror, you know, looking like a nightmare. What was real anymore? What was unreal? It was like I was caught halfway between. But the silver and red feather was still in my hands. Something, somewhere, must have been real. And a noise in my brain, nothing at all like music; altogether like a summons. A banging on my door...

People screaming down the corridors; ex-pats and earthly dreamers. They drag me from my room. The protesters have found a way through the border; now they're shuffling me outside into the field of snow. The trees are heavy with ice blossoms. The feather in my fingers, the tracks of dancers under my shoes, and the withering vision of Boogie Cops marching over the slush. The dancing people all arrested in cop-meshes. A strange crop of fruit dangling from some lonesome Tumtum tree. Original bodies, dead to the dream. Moonkeeper's corpse, just one more bruised apple, swinging. Lynch mob rhythm, pendulum style. Jodie and the Krunch, Ace and the wild 9, swinging dead from that same tree. All the love that I've ever lost, lost forever. The Jubjub birds have fluttered away into silence. The chances missed. Shadowgirl and Dogman, shadow-gone and dog-gone. My hands are tied behind my back. The feather floats away from my life. I remember a scream of livid despair rising from my throat, and then strangled by the noose that was placed around my neck, and tightened. A rope swung over a Tumtum branch. The rhythmless crowd of Boogies and Splicers and Refugees, all of them tugging on the rope...

At the last moment of my former life, one of the Boogies snatches the feather from the air. I vaguely recall the face of the highway she-cop, laughing in my face – "Choke on this, music-freak!" – as she rammed the feather into my mouth. I'm gagging on the noose and the feather, and lifted up into white heat.

Okay, like Move On Up, man; you know what I'm saying? Mayfield Demon virus to the rescue. I was let loose from the moment, totally Ian Curtis. My Dub-juicy soul floating away the dream...

I'm gagging on Moonkeeper feather. I'm flying to a new world. The dream of a dream. I'm playing edit-suite to the dead. Moon on the drums, Mingus on the bass, Hendrix on the guitar, Ian Curtis Mayfield (joined at the hip) on the vocals; myself on the controls and the all togetherness. I've been found at last.

Beat Heaven is where I'm telling this story from. I've been living here for more years than there are notes in one of Jimi's solos. The band is called The Remix Shadows. I chose that name myself, because I'm the Dub producer, and because this whole song is for Jodie and all the lost lovers of everywhere. The band is tight and the lyrics are written. I deem ourselves ready for a debut gig.

So we're coming back down to Earth. People get ready! Leave some space for the bass in your lives, and let this new disease find a home. And this time to infect only the rampant, the lustful, the nymphomatic. No more denial: I'm gonna spread my dancing juice throughout the land...

Ringpull

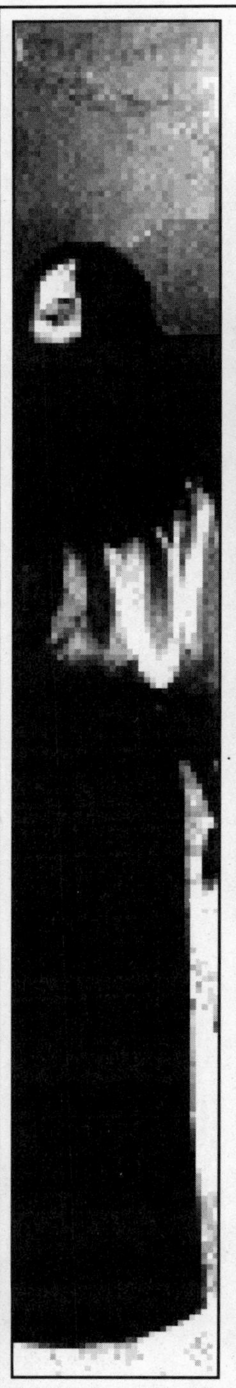

GONE

THE SMELL OF CHEMICALS FILLS THE AIR. A SAFELIGHT CRAWLS THE NORMALLY COLD TILED SPACE SPREADING A WARM GLOW. CROUCHING NAKED, HER LONG, STRAIGHT BLACK HAIR A BRUSH STROKE DOWN HER PALE BACK, SHE PADDLES WITH RUBBER TONGS IN A DEVELOPING TRAY. AN OLD-STYLE BLACK TELEPHONE SQUATS NEXT TO HER, ITS TAIL CAUGHT IN THE DOOR. SHE ROCKS THE TRAY, BREATHING THE STRANGE PERFUME, WATCHING, SMILING WICKEDLY AS THE BLACK AND WHITE PHOTOGRAPH OF A THIN NAKED MAN, SEATED ON A GRUBBY GREY CARPET AGAINST A STAINED WALL, EMERGES. COMPLAINING, THE TELEPHONE RINGS. TURNING, SHE PICKS IT UP AND SPEAKS TO HER LOVER ON THE OTHER SIDE OF THE WORLD. THE PHOTOGRAPH, FORGOTTEN, IS EXPOSED TO THE CHEMICALS FOR TOO LONG AND BURNS TO BLACKNESS.

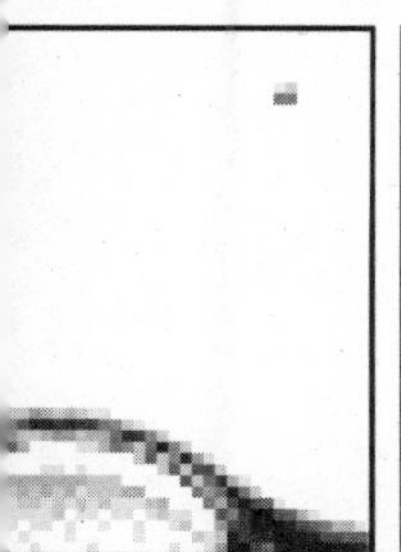

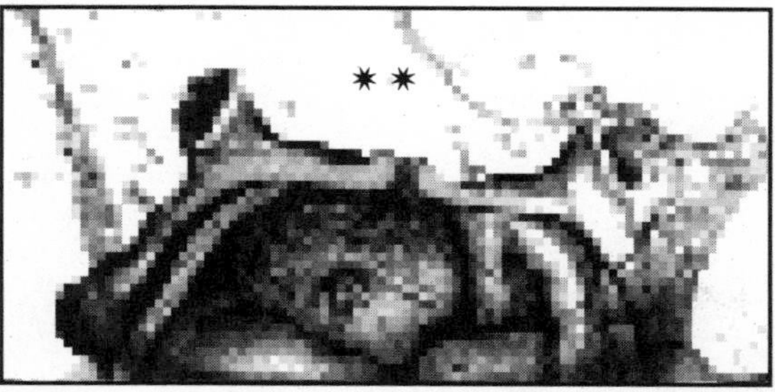

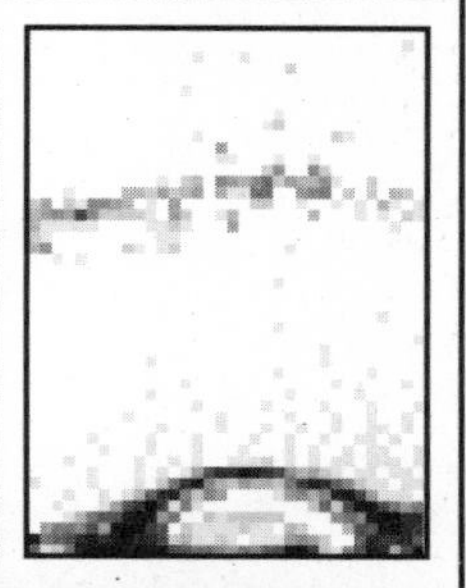

E IS LYING ON HIS BACK IN CLEAR WARM WATER.
E BREATHES EASILY, JUST BELOW THE SURFACE,
SLOW. RELAXED RHYTHM. ABOVE HIM HER FACE
PPEARS, SLIT WITH A DELICIOUSLY FERAL SMILE.
JET CASCADE FRAMES THE HAND THAT DESCENDS
O THE WATER. IT BREAKS THE SURFACE ROCKING HIM GENTLY.

SINGLE DEMANDING CHIME RAPIDLY BUILDS TO AN UNBEARABLE
EAL, TENSE, URGENT. SHE TURNS AWAY. HIS VISION IS BLURRED
Y THE RIPPLES HE HEARS A MUFFLED CONVERSATION. IT IS
NTHUSIASTIC, SURPRISED AND WARM. THE WATER
EGINS TO COOL AND THE LIGHT TO FADE LEAVING HIM
HIVERING UNCONTROLLABLY. SUDDENLY A VILE
HEMICAL STENCH GRIPS HIM. HE CAN NO
ONGER BREATH.

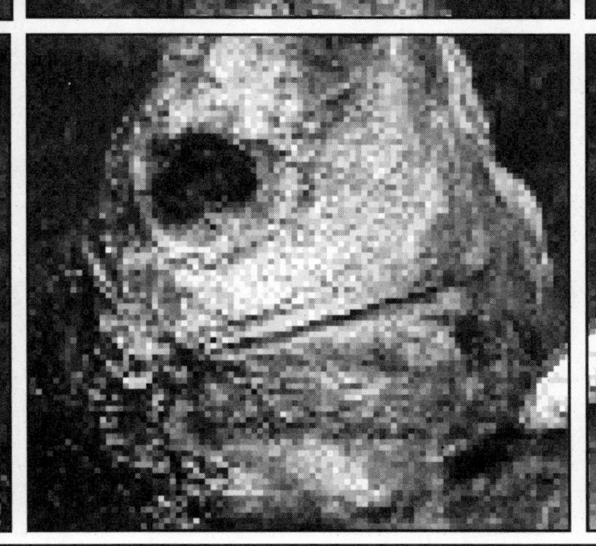

E THRASHES IN THE
ARKENING, THICKENING
IRE AS BLACKNESS
NGULFS HIM.

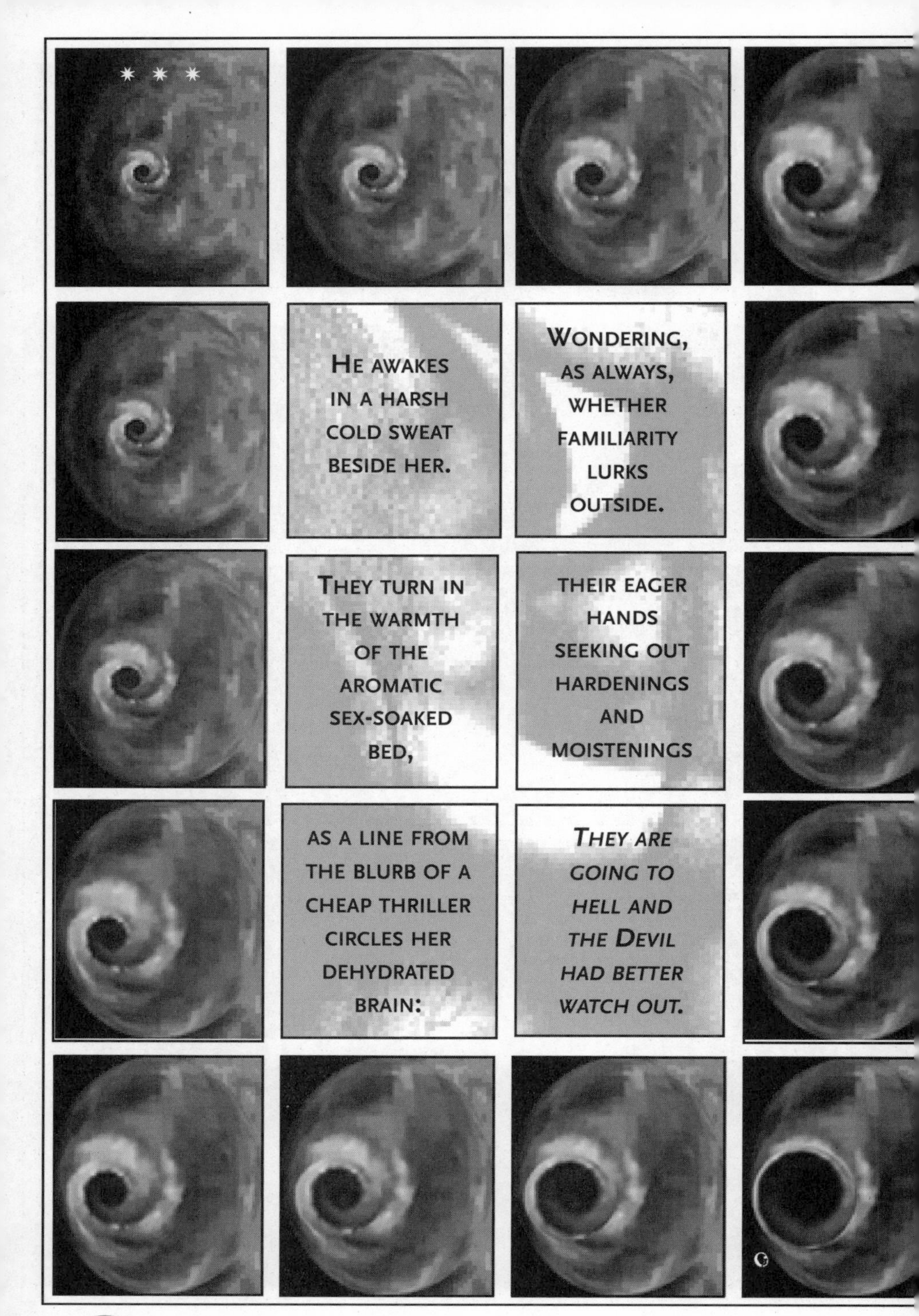
* * *
HE AWAKES IN A HARSH COLD SWEAT BESIDE HER.
WONDERING, AS ALWAYS, WHETHER FAMILIARITY LURKS OUTSIDE.
THEY TURN IN THE WARMTH OF THE AROMATIC SEX-SOAKED BED,
THEIR EAGER HANDS SEEKING OUT HARDENINGS AND MOISTENINGS
AS A LINE FROM THE BLURB OF A CHEAP THRILLER CIRCLES HER DEHYDRATED BRAIN:
THEY ARE GOING TO HELL AND THE DEVIL HAD BETTER WATCH OUT.

* * * *

I

He gave her the money she needed to get back to her lover, back to a place where she would be an outsider, but where she was at home. He gave her the envelope just as she was leaving, leaving no time for explanations.

When he arrived back he wrote a postcard he had no intention of ever sending: *I always meant to write but somehow never did, now you are gone and I'm still out here, somewhere.* He propped it up next to his bed. The telephone rang but he didn't answer it.

CALL ME

P-P. HARTNETT

extract from a novel to be published 1996

Unplugging the phone calmed me, making me feel instantly lighter.

Replying to the Welsh git's ad was proving to be one of those classic big mistakes. I shouldn't have given him my surname, shouldn't have let slip where my parents lived. I gave him too much information. The consequences were rattling, mostly under my skin.

I've never had a problem with my Yamaha, having to refer to the trouble shooting page in the owner's guide but that day there was no sound and I couldn't work out why. It took me an hour to realise that the MASTER VOLUME was on zero. I was pissed off about it but glad that I'd managed to work out the mystery problem alone.

Arriving at a LO TOM which I slowed right down, pressing

SUSTAIN I started, playing simple root chords using the slap bass sound. Seeing that my fingertips were turning white, I realised I was fingering with excessive force which could have damaged the terminals. Deciding to abandon any idea of making some sort of recording, I switched off the power supply then plugged the phone back in which was an odd thing to do as it was bedtime. The phone started ringing as plug entered socket.

Considering disconnection, just for a moment, I entered a dilemma. I couldn't resist lifting the receiver. There were no words, just long-distance crackle and grit, then the line went dead. Pip. Him again.

In raised capitals, gold on creamy yellow, one word:

ALWAYS

D

The slanted single initial was larger than any of those before.

If it hadn't been me it would have been someone else. Dai needed a point of focus and I just happened to be the one around at the time. Not many young men would have bought the man a cup of tea unless paid a pretty good hourly rate.

He didn't need *me*, he needed *something* to make up for the long years of loneliness, the difficulty of being a silent queer. Pre '67 was one thing, the disco '70s another. He was ugly and didn't fit in. He couldn't cope, had no strategies, no support network. One of the bravest things he ever did was place a dumb ad in *The Pink Paper*. The desperate sodomite, he wanted much more than his money's worth from that box number.

His self-esteem was rock bottom. Friendless, boyfriendless, stuck in the job rut. Someone always on the sidelines of life. (Always the difficulty of cooking a meal for one,

always the awkwardness at social events.) Family affairs had frayed him. (Always the same old flat, same old armchair, those slippers. Tears on the bed each Sunday.)
I really should have phoned the old fool.

He felt powerless until he started the adoration reversal routine.

Friendship cards are both big business and a pain in the arse. Feeling strangely drawn to do a spot of market research, I entered Paperchase purposefully.

Graphic: A bridge.
Wording outside: ***Cross Over The Bridge To Me***
Wording inside: ***Be Mine***

Graphic: A love heart.
Wording outside: ***I LOVE YOU*** written maybe twenty times
Wording inside: ***...and the amazing thing is we've just met!***

Graphic: Infantile smiley face.
Wording outside: ***Thinking Of You***
Wording inside: ***Puts A Smile On My Face!***

Graphic: Clouds.
Wording outside: ***YOU...*** in creamy yellow on palest blue.
Wording inside: ***You Are A Part Of Everything I Do...***

Graphic: A lacey pillow case.
Wording outside: ***Even When We're Apart...***
Wording inside: ***I Sleep With You In My Heart...***

Graphic: Two words in four different font styles.
Wording outside: ***I Care***
Wording inside: ***I'm Always There...***

Graphic: Flames.
Wording outside: ***Hell...***
Wording inside: ***O!***

And there were many, many more, waiting to be signed, sealed and delivered. I felt decidedly light-headed in there, watching the punters making up their minds.

The long-distance crackle and grit went on for longer than usual. It sounded so much clearer than the answerphone recordings. He was breathing like a bull. A little girl could be heard way off in the distance, screaming. Little birds too. I'd been expecting the call and nine o'clock on a Sunday morning was his chosen time to speak. (Sundays can be so difficult, what with building sites stilled and couples in casuals everywhere.)

After years of immobilisation, stunned by romantic obsession, wanting but not getting (and a whole lot more), he was angry. I imagined him as an adolescent, using fantasy and compulsive masturbation as fun, then as a distraction, then to avoid feelings or as a reward or just boredom's time filler.

"I gave you my number. You could've called me. I think you should've called - don't you?" Each clipped syllable had the clarity of threat. Here was yet another specimen illustrating the variety, diversity and desperation of gay life.

"You're out a lot, aren't you lad? I've spent a fortune listening to your answerphone message."

A countdown had begun with the arrival of the ***Living Card*** Interflora had delivered weeks back. I was close to the most thrilling part of a countdown, I'd reached ten.

10

"I bet you've been slagging your arse up and down Old Compton Street or in some sauna."

9

"bet you've been out dipping your wick, haven't you lad?"

8

"I hope you wore a condom."

7

"I'm a decent, respectable, good, clean-living man and you're not interested."

6

"You know what you are...and you should probably note this down..."

5

"You're nothing but a hopeless, heartless little whore."

4

"A shaggable, shaggable little tart, whore, queer."

3

(A remarkably accurate assessment, delivered in a somewhat melodramatic tone. Nicely put, though, I thought, venting all the UK's bitterness since the Domesday Book. I noted the definition down, complying with the gentleman's suggestion.)

2

"You bastard!"

1

"You fucking deceiver you."

0

"I'll have your guts for garters!" he peaked.

BLAST OFF

"I only wanted us to be friends."

He wanted us to be lovers - and if we couldn't be lovers then we couldn't be friends. This happens.

My telephone manner became very Chinese take-away, saying as little as possible with an emphasis on good manners. Hoping to swot him down with silence, I exercised perfect facial immobility. Beginning to sincerely hope this man would end his days in an M3 pile up - the sooner the better - I blew my cool.

"Tell me...*(pause)*...is there any history of...*(slightest pause)*...insanity in your family?"
His little breathing difficulty increased with the slap of sarcasm.

"Now there's no need to get nasty," he whined.

After a little difficulty with both grip of the handset and formation of a word beginning with 'y', he managed to blurt, "*Y*-You little whore!"

I found the pronunciation of this interesting, delivered like *who-were*. His volume, however, lacked impact. In the silence that followed, I imagined him with a probation teacher's dick in his mouth, then a gun, then both - shooting. To make him really blow his top I gave him my usual standard stupid question, getting up his arse the way I like to.

"What do you reckon Joe Orton was reincarnated as?" I asked, perhaps just a little like a satirical game-show host.

"A queer little slag like you I should think," he retorted with admirable speed.
I felt somewhat honoured and maybe he sensed my smile in the silence.

"Believe me," he said in the tone of a Tower Hamlets supply teacher, "I'll have you, you young bugger!"

"Yes, I heard. Guts for garters, I think you said. Must fax

that to Jean Paul Gaultier."

He slammed the phone down.

Ten minutes later the phone rang, perhaps up to a full minute. I ignored it.

Twenty minutes later the phone rang four times, then stopped.
Thirty minutes later the phone rang twice, stopped.
Forty five minutes later the phone rang just the once,
a little tring to say: ***Thinking Of You.***

shooting up

a retrospective exhibition of nightclub and street-style documentation by p-p. hartnett

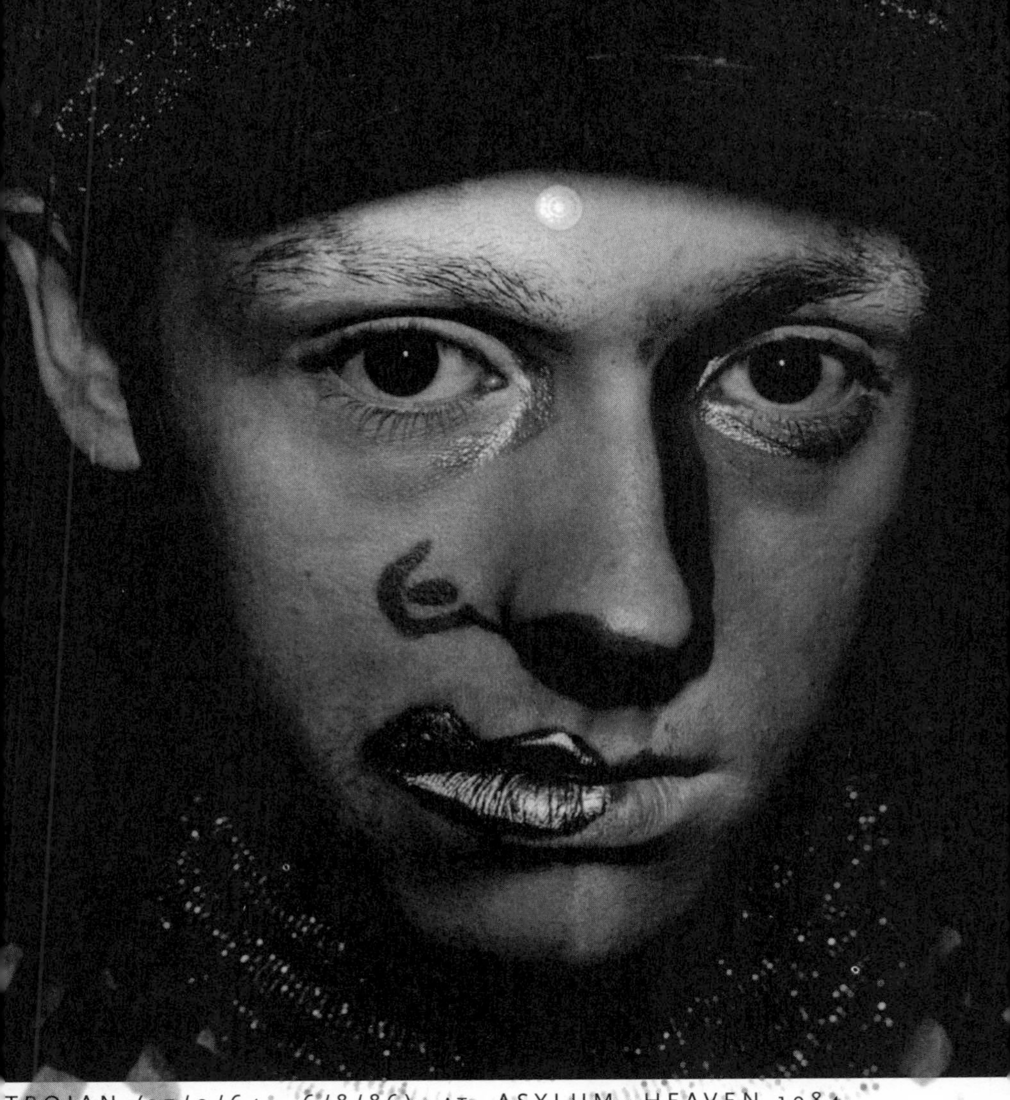

TROJAN (17/9/64 - 6/8/86), AT ASYLUM, HEAVEN 1984

at THE ORIGINAL LEVI'S® STORE
LEVI'S GALLERY 174-176 REGENT STREET LONDON W1
0171 439 2014

3-29 NOVEMBER 1995

a pagan day

TONY WHITE

The day after boxing day 1984, Jesus was in William's room drinking tea and smoking a joint. Jesus's real name was Trevor, but he'd been called Jesus ever since he had a conversation with a higher being one evening as he watched the sunset over Pudsey. Jesus was the original crusty. It was he who, when I saw him in the summer of 1985 and asked, 'Is that your dog?', said, 'Yes and he's not wearing a collar because he's a friend and not a slave.'

We had been listening to the new Psychic TV album A PAGAN DAY. With the exception of side one, track four, COLD STEEL (which is a version of THE ORCHIDS, side one, track two of DREAMS LESS SWEET, but with vocals by Fergusson instead of P-Orridge)
A PAGAN DAY consisted largely of several very simple new tracks featuring drum machine, guitar and keyboards: like a slightly less benign Young Marble Giants. A PAGAN DAY was undoubtedly Psychic TV's best album. It was also a picture disc: the A side of the record features a colour photo of one time performance artist and Throbbing Gristle front man Genesis P-Orridge's daughter Caresse.

I took the album off the turntable and returned it to its clear plastic sleeve, then read the track listings which constituted the 'picture' on the B side of the disc.

25 DECEMBER 1984
A PAGAN DAY
PSYCHIC TV

SIDE ONE
1. CADAQUES
2. WE KISS
3. OPIUM
4. COLD STEEL
5. L.A.
6. ICELAND

SIDE TWO
1. TRANSLUCENT CARRIAGES
2. PARIS
3. BABY'S GONE AWAY
4. ALICE
5. NEW SEXUALITY

© 1984 Temple Records TOPY 003
Published by Crippled Frog Music 1984

Released 11 am 24th December 1984
Deleted 12 am 24th December 1984

All songs and music by Alex Fergusson
and Genesis P-Orridge except 'Translucent Carriages'
which is a song by the enigmatic Tom Rapp

For the realisation of this project
Psychic TV were:
ALEX FERGUSSON & GENESIS P-ORRIDGE.
PHOTO OF CARESSE BY ANDREW RAWLING
LIMITED EDITION OF 999 COPIES

So Jesus, then, had promised to take William and myself out to the moors to see the 'Swastika Stone', which was some sort of, perhaps, neolithic or Iron Age stone with, Jesus said, a *swastika* carved on it. I couldn't quite picture this but it seemed like a good idea for a day out.

Jesus wasn't tripping that day but it hardly made any difference. His planned substance intake for the day, our supplies, consisted of a jar of honey and a brown paper bag full of Kava Kava, a stimulant which was apparently derived from the bark of some South Pacific tree. I decided that Jesus was using the term 'derived from' rather loosely: as far as I could tell the stuff in the bag *was* the bark of a tree. Anyway, thus prepared we took the bus out to Ilkley.

J e s u s   w a s

p r e t t y

s p a c e d   o u t

a l r e a d y.

He started talking about Ley Lines, those druidic highways linking stone circles and other mystic sites. The journey from the centre of Leeds to Ilkley took about an hour. Jesus, looking out of the window, started to read the road signs aloud. 'Otley 10 miles, Batley 30 miles, Shipley 20 miles, Ilkley 15 miles.' And, by putting an emphasis on the last syllable of each town, he indicated to us an important discovery which he had made, perhaps, on some previous trip to the Swastika Stone. Like some Glastonbury of the North, this part of Yorkshire was wearing its pagan heart on its sleeve. What could 'Otley' mean but *the Ley Line of Ot.* Batley, Shipley, Ilkley, it was there for all to see.

The rest of the journey saw Jesus staring out of the window lost in his thoughts. Scratch the surface of these West Yorkshire towns and you find a teeming web of energy. Presumably the Swastika Stone was also a major intersection on this vast and mystic network.
A convoy of Police vans sped past the bus.

. . . .

Eventually we arrived at Ilkley and headed straight out of town. The wind was blowing down over the edge of the moor, but we were well wrapped up and pulled our hats down around our ears. I was wearing a sort of denim fisherman's cap which I'd bought in the indoor market in Newcastle. Jesus was wearing a 'Benny' type woollen hat and William was wearing a trilby which he'd been given by some guy called Ghengis.

At this point I had not met Ghengis, but before the week was out on New Years Day 1985, there was a knock on the door. I was watching some Super 8 films but went and answered the door.

He was really William's friend, but William was out. He seemed like a total fucking nutter though, so I said, 'Come in anyway and have a cup of tea'. I was feeling rather devil-may-care, having just found and ingest-ed around half of the preceding autumn's leftover magic mushrooms.

He stayed all day. At least it seemed like all day. Then William came back and Ghengis said 'Hey listen lads, I'm moving down to London tomorrow so I'm sort of clearing out me flat like. Bring some rubbish bags round in a bit and you can tek ought you want.' Then he left. We thought it might be quite a laugh and there might even be some records, so we grabbed a couple of black bin liners and walked over.

It was terrible being there, tripping, picking over all this rubbish in some dingy little flat off Victoria Road while Ghengis said things like, 'No, go on tek it, I want to give it to me mates'. It was hard to keep a straight face. I came away with a broken hand drill and a personal stereo that was held together with insulating tape and William got a crap leather jacket and some other shit that I can't remember. As soon as we got out of the door we just burst out laughing and laughed all the way home, running through the slush with our bin bags.

That night we were supposed to be going to a party. William went on ahead and I said I would come along in a bit. I took all the remaining mushrooms before I left, then walked to the party, listening to A PAGAN DAY on Ghengis's personal stereo.

By the time I got there I was really tripping, so much so that I couldn't talk. Arthur's girlfriend Nancy, whose mother was in the same Psychiatric Hospital as Eddie Waring, was trying to match me up with one of her friends while I was having all these stupid hallucinations. I picked up some DIY book of how to make felt dinosaur toys. I thought it was how to make beer mats with pictures of felt dinosaur toys on them. And it might have been that I'd had such an odd day showing Ghengis my Super 8 films over and over and then going to his drab little flat, but I couldn't speak and it seemed like we were in a bubble floating high above the night time city and I wanted to be part of the night time city. I wanted to be part of the day time city. Any city. At that moment I lost my previously unshakeable faith in the truly visionary potential of hallucinogenic drugs.

But I stayed until everyone else had gone, watching Mickey Mouse playing the piano on the walls. Then William and I walked home.

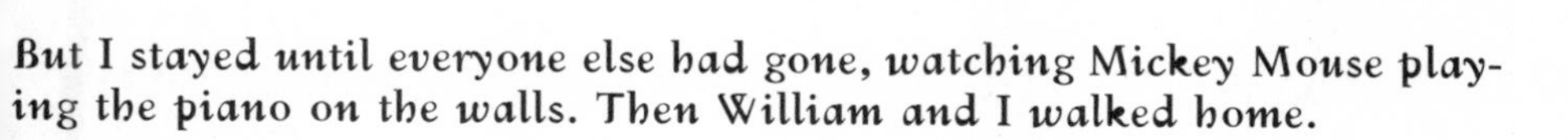

Jesus, William and I trudged on across the moors. After a while, Jesus got out the bag of Kava Kava and we scooped lumps into the honey and chewed on it. It was impossible to tell whether this woody pulp was having any stimulating effect, but it was a nice idea and seemed to promise us a degree of internal warmth so we carried on, occasionally braving the cold to roll cigarettes which we smoked in cupped hands to shield the end from the wind.

It took longer than we'd thought to get to the Swastika Stone. The wind was still cutting across the moors and as we climbed over fences and stiles we noticed that there was a thick layer of ice on the lee-ward side of all the fence wires.

We eventually found it. There was an iron railing on the edge of the moor, on the very edge of the steep escarpment. This was a three sided enclosure, obviously the missing fourth side was beyond the edge of the

cliff and there were fans of spiked railings which projected further out into the swirling mist. Inside this small enclosure was a squarish rock, the swastika stone itself, and outside sat a replica, cast from the original. After such a long walk the idea that we might be satisfied with a quick look at this replica and then be on our way, seemed almost like an insult. We wanted to squat around the stone like it was a table. We wanted to run our fingers across that scarred surface and have some kind of intimate contact with it. So we climbed out over the edge of the cliff, around the spikes and into the enclosure.

We could now clearly see the swastika and it was nothing like the Hindu/Nazi swastika. It was like two swirly 'S's interlocking and the ends of each 'S' curled right round to form four little circles and in the centre of each of these four circles was a dot. From the tip of one of these 'S's curled another smaller comma shape, again with a dot in its centre. It was good. We ran our fingers down the ancient grooves and felt ... cold.

. . . .

Soon after New Year, William had a breakdown. I suppose that's what it was. Something happened and whatever it was he changed fundamentally. I first realised something was wrong when we were in my room listening to the limited edition live album NEW YORK SCUM HATERS (1984, TEMPLE RECORDS, TOPY 002), and when Genesis P-Orridge sang the chorus of one of the songs, William looked at me and said, 'I thought it went "humiliation based on skinhead interrogation."' He was terrified. Whenever I saw him there was just this look of absolute terror on his face. He thought that he was under surveillance and that someone was changing the lyrics of all these familiar records.

Things came to a head at a New Order gig at The Ritzy Ballroom in the Merrion Centre on 27th January. We had booked tickets for this gig long before Christmas. POWER, CORRUPTION AND LIES was seldom off William's record player.

There was some awful support band on when we arrived and most of our friends were already there. I stood and chatted to them for a while but William was really nervous and stalked around. I thought that perhaps I should make conversation or something, so I said, half-joking, 'Christ this band's awful, who the hell are they?' He looked at me with this haunted expression and said, 'Isn't it New Order?' Then he paused for a second, said: 'I think I should go,' and turned and walked out of The Ritzy. I think it was then that we all realized that something was very wrong, so the next day we rang his parents and they came straight over and collected him.

But, apart from that, it was a great gig. It was brilliant hearing so much electronic noise in the slightly incongruous surroundings of the Ritzy, where the decor was designed to resemble some kind of generic South Sea island: Kava Kava might have been a more appropriate intoxicant than half pints of cheap lager in plastic glasses. They did Blue Monday and Temptation as well as the newer stuff. Oliver had his Walkman and taped it. I'd heard that New Order were a really bad live band, that they played short sets and didn't do encores. But I guess we were lucky because that day was Gillian's birthday and the whole audience sang Happy Birthday which put them in a good mood and they did two encores. Oliver passed his bootleg on to Len (the tape-worm) who sorted the EQ out a bit and made us all copies.

. . . .

But that was all in the future. For now, on Ilkley Moor, Jesus was proud to have shown us the Swastika Stone and ceremoniously unscrewed the lid from the jar of honey. He placed the jar on the centre of the stone. We each took a big woody lump of Kava Kava from the bag and dipped it into the honey, chewing heartily before clambering back out into space, clinging onto the icy railings and swinging ourselves back onto the cliff edge.

Stumbling back along the barely visible track through the freezing mist in twilight, we decided that, rather than walk back towards Ilkley, we should go on to Addingham which was nearer, and get a bus from there. Within minutes we had stumbled off the track, but Jesus trudged on, chewing his Kava Kava, and we followed. After about forty minutes of terror in the fog, we found another path which became a track which became a road which eventually led us to Addingham and a pint of Tetleys each in front of the fire, before catching the bus home.

fishtank

ELAINE PALMER

Sava cries a lot lately. Not about having a baby, that isn't real. She worries about stretch marks and cries over silly things like people skipping the queue in front of her at the supermarket.

At four months when Sava saw the swirling blue dots, she had a rush of warm feeling towards the little video blob. The nurse pressed the sensor into the cold gel on her belly, and the thing onscreen tried to wriggle away. They showed her its head, negatived like a skull. Sava said it was gruesome and the nurse asked "where's your maternal instinct?" After that came a guided tour of various body parts. Sava couldn't decode the images, they were just a blur of bluewhite dots, a pulsing submarine shape.

Later, she remembered the nurse saying: "look how he's swimming" and "see his tiny hands." Sava thought *Hey*, it's a boy!
When Sava's friend had twins, she thought Tania just *would* have baby boys. Tania had had so

many lovers that Franco, her husband, still cried when he thought about them. Now he'd be jealous all over again.
At school, Tania had been first to wear a bra and smoke cigarettes; later, she deflowered boys as a hobby. Sava always wanted to be like her but was scared to let it happen. So she was kind of shocked after the scan, to be a bit like Tania after all.

The big black family album is full of Sava's older brother, Joey: Joey asleep in his carry-cot, Joey on a rug in the back garden, Joey with all the grown-ups gathered round adoringly.
"Where are *my* baby photos?" Sava asks her mother.
"Well, look, you're in that one aren't you, and that." She points out Sava behind or beside Joey.
"Don't you have any proper ones of me, like this?" She flips back to the large professional portraits in feint flaky colours.
"Oh, I don't remember," Sava's mother says, going back to her magazine. "You could look in the garage I suppose."
In the old paint-spattered dresser where Sava's father hoards screwdrivers, pliers, nuts and bolts, one drawer is stuffed with reject prints and negative bags. Sava sifts through them, but still can't find any photographs of herself as a baby. There are plenty of her and her brother as toddlers, playing on black and white Cornish beaches. In these later pictures, Sava wears big cheesy smiles, neatly brushed hair and freshly ironed dresses. Joey squints at their father behind the camera or looks away, bored, his hair blowing over his eyes.

Sava and TeeJay went on holiday and tried to forget. They had romantic dinners in riverside restaurants, and asked strangers to photograph the two of them like it was the last time they'd ever be together. Each night they stopped at the bridge on the way back to the hotel, and watched the lights reflected in the soupy black water.
TeeJay took a photo of Sava on the beach, belly rounding out her swimsuit. She wrote a postcard to her parents:
Dear Mum & Dad. Having a nice time. Weather great. By the way, baby due September.
Sava passed the card to TeeJay, who scribbled: *TeeJay probable father.*

TeeJay has a dream about the baby. Sava thinks this is a sign he's getting used to the idea, and asks what happened in his dream.
Somehow the baby has got up on the roof. TeeJay's worried it will try to fly down again. "It's so stupid," he says, "it might like the idea of floating on air." He wants to climb up and rescue it but he can't find a ladder.

"So what happened?" Sava asks.
"Well, that's when I woke up," TeeJay says, but Sava's not sure she believes him.
"How did the baby get up there in the first place?" she asks.
"Oh, I don't know, you left it there probably," TeeJay says.
The sea's dead glassy as the plane drops over the English coast. There's been a major heatwave in their absence. London's dried to a crisp, sticky as an ice lolly wrapper.

The phone was ringing as they unlocked the door. It was Sava's mother, wanting to know when Sava and TeeJay were getting married.
Finally Sava got her off the phone.
"I knew I shouldn't have told her," she said. "Now I can't change my mind and have it adopted. At least I gave her a fake due date, so we'll have a few days peace."
"You what?" Theoretically, TeeJay was on better terms with his mother, who lived a very long way away. He saw her every five years or so, and he hadn't even told her Sava was pregnant.
Sava's mother rang back. She'd been thinking, with Joey taking so long to come out of his rebellious gay phase, perhaps it wasn't such bad news after all. She thought she could come to terms with it, in time. And she was really looking forward to becoming a grandmother. Sava passed the phone to TeeJay, and went to bed.

"We'll have to get it a game-boy before it hits school," TeeJay says.
Sava looks at him. "It's nice of you to take an interest, but I don't know if a gameboy's a good idea. Especially for a boy."
"C'mon, you want it to be socially inept like all the other kids, don't you?" TeeJay says. "I mean you know how important conformity is at that age."

A conciliatory parcel arrived. "I expect you've got lots of baby things already," said the letter. "When Joey was born I had enough

for at least two babies."
In fact Sava and TeeJay had bought nothing. It seemed weird, buying clothes for someone you'd never met. What if they didn't fit?
In the parcel was a blue one-piece suit with a teddy motif. Sava held it up to her tummy. It couldn't possibly be that big, she decided.

"I'm thinking of getting my hair cut," Sava says, the week before she's due. "It might not be practical having it long. The baby's bound to pull at it."
TeeJay's watching the X-Files. He waits until an ad break comes up before saying: "Look, if it pulls your hair, you should tell it to fuck off or move out. I get a pretty raw deal around here, why should it get special treatment?"

When Sava woke up and looked in the fishtank, she thought the baby must have been switched.
"It was meant to be a boy. They *said* when I had the scan."
"Scans aren't definitive, you know," TeeJay said.
"What do you know? Besides, it doesn't look like either of us."
"I should hope not. It's like something off Star Trek. Or Doctor Who. Anyhow, I was watching while you were asleep, and no-one switched it. We're stuck with this one, they don't do refunds."
TeeJay scooped the baby out of the tank. It stared at him and wiggled its fingers.

TECHNOPAGAN – THE AUTHORS

CITY OF FUSION
nicholas royle's first novel *counterparts* is published by penguin. his second book, *saxaphone dreams*, is due in 1996

stationary
sonya aurora madan is lead vocalist and songwriter with echobelly

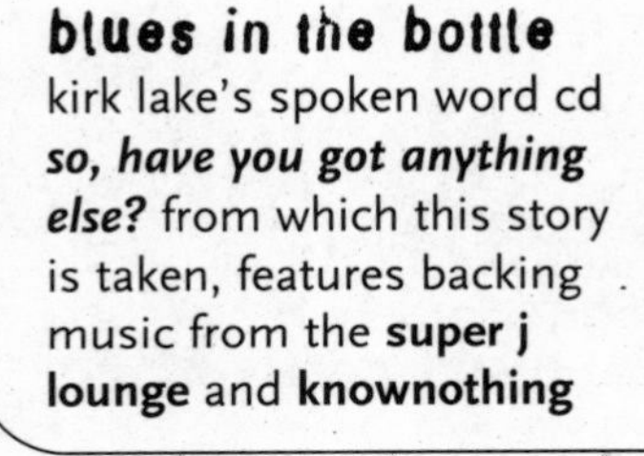

blues in the bottle
kirk lake's spoken word cd ***so, have you got anything else?*** from which this story is taken, features backing music from the **super j lounge** and **knownothing**

pecan pie
sarah jane contributed a longer story, *brigitte bardot*, to the pulp faction compilation *SKIN*

ELASTIC ETHER
scanner (robin rimbaud) makes a living scavenging the airwaves.
elastic ether is based on tape-recordings of real mobile phone conversations

selling sweatshirts on venice beach
ralph dartford lives in essex

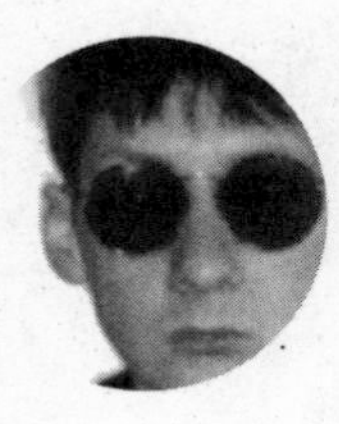

repeater
steve aylett works as a belching consultant on the outskirts of trumpton. his books *the crime studio* and *bigot hall* are published by serif

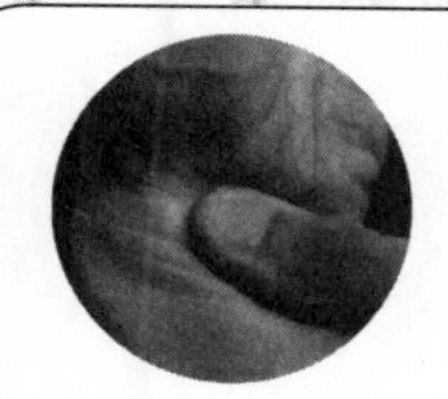

drive – in

m dawes is a visual and performance artist of obscure gender who lives in glasgow

RUSH

simon lewis has vanished, possibly to china.

planting seeds

hilaire

scat

darren francis plays keyboards with techno-metal band *cubanate*. his short novel *skin of my dead mother* was published by pulp faction in *SKIN*

PERFORMANCE DEATH

penny j cotton works for a drugs and legal advice agency

GONE

ralph mepham

artificially induced dub syndrome

jeff noon's acclaimed books *vurt* and *pollen* are published by ringpull. *dub syndrome* is his first fictional trip out of manchester

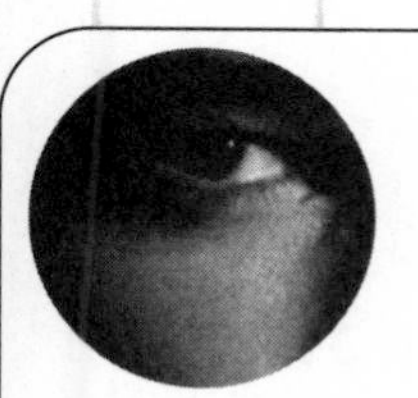

call me

p-p. hartnett is a photographer, and runs the london club for drag kings, naive. his début novel, *call me*, is to be published in 1996

a pagan day

tony white is an artist and lives in london's east end

fishtank

elaine palmer edited *SKIN* and *TECHNOPAGAN*, both published by pulp faction 1995

SKIN

20 stories from new and challenging writers. Contributing authors include Barry Adamson, ex-THE BAD SEEDS, and Darren Francis, keyboards player with cult techno band CUBANATE.

"Compelling imagery and ideas"
TIME OUT

March 1995 Fiction £5.99 128 pages ISBN 1 899571 00 0

TECHNOPAGAN

TECHNOPAGAN's themes are the media, music and technology and how they cohabit and clash with human needs and desires. Contributing authors include Jeff Noon, Nicholas Royle, Sonya of Echobelly, Scanner, Steve Aylett, Kirk Lake, Darren Francis.

November 1995 Fiction £6.99 128 pages ISBN 1 899571 01 9

HOMELANDS

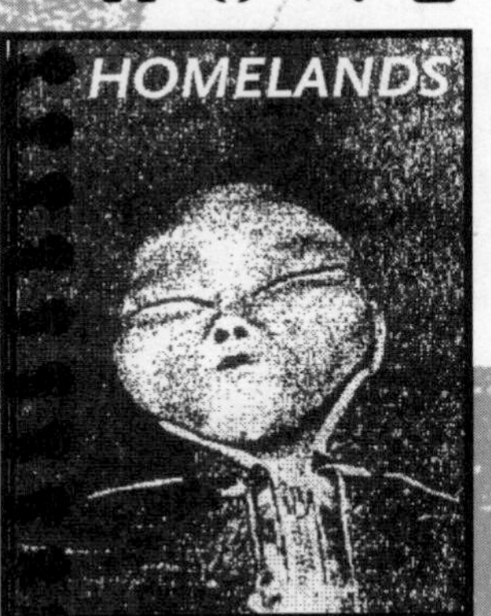

Due out in early 1996, HOMELANDS takes a fresh look at the fertile territory of living space and relationships, nuclear and non. Expect the unexpected.

February 1996 Fiction £6.99 128 pages ISBN 1 899571 02 7

WANTED: NEW WRITING

Pulp Faction publishes new writers in its series of fiction compilations. The titles can be seen by contributors as a starting point – they are open to creative interpretation and to infiltration by non-themed items.
Stories from 750 to 3,000 words may be sent at any time.
Unused manuscripts returned only if suitable SAE attached.

Send text (typed, A4) and/or images to:
The Editors, Pulp Faction,
60 Alexander Road, London, N19 3PQ
.*NEXT DEADLINE*: Fission, 1 Feb 1996 (published July 1996).

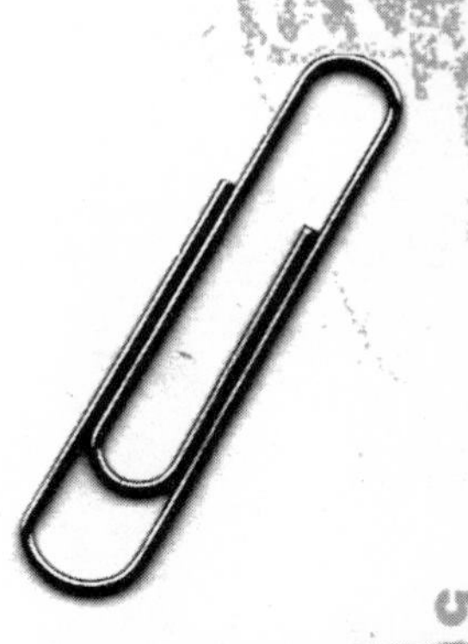